The Escape

Nightfall, Book Four

Cynthia Melton

DEDICATION

To my loyal readers who eagerly await the next book.

1

I glanced over my shoulder at Fawke, his face serious, then back at the monitor in front of me. While we'd found other refugees from Soriah in the tunnels surrounding our underground compound, it surprised me to see a healthy someone out in the open. The young man wore simple but clean clothes and didn't appear to carry a weapon.

"Widen the view." I peered closer as the drone footage widened.

Fawke Newton leaned over my shoulder smelling of soap from his recent shower. "Crynn Dayholt, those buildings look lived in." He pointed to a cluster of structures where clothing flapped from a line, chickens roamed the streets, and a child dashed from one building to another.

"They don't seem to be afraid of malignants at all." How could that be? To be out in the open was a death sentence as many of Soriah's soldiers were finding out. As I'd found out my first day outside the white walls as leader of the Stalkers, a fate chosen for me on my eighteenth birthday. A day that seemed much further back than a year ago.

"That's why." He drew my attention to a deep trench around the perimeter of the "city." "Not even a malignant can jump that. They have a drawbridge."

The city was more like a town or a village considering the few buildings. How many residents? A hundred?

As the drone continued its flight, gardens appeared, a few pens of livestock, and a man who looked very much in charge. He marched to the side of the young man we'd spotted first and stared up at the drone. For several minutes his features remained hard, impassive, then they spread into a smile as he waved for us to come.

"Bring the drone back." Until we knew whether we could trust this group, we didn't need them following the drone we'd sent out to scout for nests of malignants.

The survivors we'd discovered in the tunnels had joined us. Our group grew in number but still wasn't large enough to take on the city of Soriah. Perhaps this new group could also be trusted.

"What are you thinking?" Fawke straightened.

"Do we pay them a visit? The trip would take two days at the least. Three if we run into trouble."

"We haven't been out of the compound in a few weeks. A searching trip might do us good." He crossed his arms and perched against the edge of the desk. "We still need fighters for the upcoming war. That means we have to ask the people we find to join us."

"True." I turned from the now dark monitor. Truth be told, I could use a day outside. Perhaps I'd get the chance to kill a malignant or two. No matter how many we killed, there always seemed to be more. We'd spent our time lately keeping up with our training, so heading out wouldn't be a great danger.

How had this new group kept the creatures away long enough to dig a trench as deep and wide as the one the drone revealed? I cast a sideways glance at Fawke. "What if they can't be trusted?"

"We keep the location of this compound secret until we know. If we don't feel as if we can trust them, we'll simply leave them be." With a smile, he cupped my cheeks. "You've never been this hesitant before."

"Something in that man's eyes bothered me. Like a shark's eyes I'd seen in a book once."

He chuckled. "I'll be with you the whole time. Come on." He straightened. "Let's find the others and get their input. It's time for the midday meal anyway."

Nodding, I followed him to the dining room where our original group sat around the same table. Despite the months we'd lived in the compound, they still preferred each other's company to that of the other residents. The new exception was sixteen-year-old, Jerome, who refused to not be a part of the group. The teen considered himself a seasoned warrior.

"You guys aren't ones for mingling." I headed for the food line where I received a sandwich of bread, mystery meat, and some kind of spread.

"Anyone tasted this yet?" I asked, taking my seat.

"I've had worse." Dante wrinkled his nose. "I think it's rat. We've plenty of them around."

Ezra took a big bite of his sandwich. "Can't be too picky while living underground, folks." His gaze searched both my and Fawke's face. "What's up?"

I explained about what the drone had found. "We're thinking of heading out."

"You say they're living there with livestock and such?" Dante's dark forehead creased. "In the open? What about Soriah?"

I shrugged. "That's a question we can ask once we get there. Who's willing?"

Everyone nodded.

"The infirmary is empty." Kira wiped her mouth with the back of her hand. "Nothing keeping me here right now. It'll be good to take the old group out."

"And me." Jerome frowned. "No way I'm staying behind. I'm one of you now."

Fawke rubbed the boy's head. "Wouldn't dream of leaving you behind. You've become quite the fighter." He met my gaze and smiled.

"Of course, we couldn't." Jerome had proven himself time and again. The boy was more skilled at fighting at the age of sixteen than I'd been at eighteen. Still, the group did their best to keep him away from heavy fighting. "Can everyone be ready to leave at dark? Once we approach the edge of their city, we'll hole up until light. Lars can guide us using the drone."

Again, multiple heads bobbed, excitement shining on every face. It appeared as if Fawke and I weren't the only ones with cabin fever. "I'll go say goodbye to my mother and meet up with all of you in the supply room an hour before nightfall."

"I'll let the kitchen know we'll need supplies." Gage headed in the direction of the food line.

I found Mom where she usually spent her time—in the infirmary. She glanced up from rolling bandages and grinned, then her smile faded. "You're going out, Crynn, aren't you?"

"How do you always know what I'm thinking?" I gave her a quick hug before sitting in a nearby chair.

"Because I'm your mother." She stashed the bandages in a cupboard. "I'm guessing Kira is going with you?" At my nod, she started pulling items from storage. "You'll need supplies. Tell me where you're going."

I again explained what the drone had shown us. "I agree with Fawke that we can't ignore potential fighters."

"Why hasn't Soriah attacked them?"

"Maybe for the same reason the malignants are kept out. That moat is pretty impressive."

"Hmm." She faced me. "I haven't been gone from Soriah for long. It doesn't seem possible they'd leave people alone. If they found this place, they'd destroy each and every one of us."

"Yes, but maybe they don't see these others as a threat. We're rebels, Mom. We've killed Soriah soldiers, taken others captive. They should be worried about us." We were bringing a war to their doorsteps.

Mom handed me a backpack full of medical

supplies. "Do you want me to have the kitchen pack food?"

"That's being taken care of. Thanks."

A sad smile graced her face. "What happened to my little girl who loved nothing more than to bury her nose in a book?"

"She turned eighteen and had to spin the wheel." I planted a kiss on her cheek. "See you in a few days."

"Promise?"

"Promise." I smiled and strolled back into the hall, hoping, praying I could keep my promise.

Mom had already undertaken a lot by fleeing Soriah. After witnessing her friends torn apart by the monsters who roamed the streets outside, she didn't need to lose her only child.

My next stop was the room I shared with Fawke. There, I packed a bag for a few days' travel before heading to the storage room for weapons. By the time I arrived, the others were gathering. It seemed everyone wanted to get a head start so as to be prepared for nightfall.

"Sword is sharpened." Moses tossed me the one that felt like an extension of myself. "Take your pick of guns. All are ready to go."

Although I preferred the sword, I grabbed a holster with a handgun, shoved a rifle into my pack, and stuffed a dagger into each boot. "Ready as I can be."

Lars entered the room with earpieces for everyone. "Keep these in and on. I can't communicate with you unless you do." He handed each of us one. "The monitors will be running. There will be a drone leading you and another patrolling the area. If danger comes too close, you'll know in plenty of time to be prepared. Except—" He sighed. "There are parts of this city where we still haven't installed cameras, and we don't have good reception for the drones. Move carefully."

I nodded, knowing of the areas he spoke about. We'd traveled through them any times. "We'll be on constant guard. Any news on Soriah's army?"

"You'll run across some patrols, but nothing major. The malignants keep them close to camp. Since we've not caused them any trouble lately, they seem to have stopped searching for us."

"Which will make our journey easier." Fawke strapped on a double-holster belt, then he chose a military-style rifle.

Ezra joined us. "Food supplies and riot gear are waiting by the entrance. We'll all be loaded. Seems like too much stuff for only a couple of days."

"We might need something to soften the mood of those we're going to see." Fawke grinned. "Food is always a good thing to have too much of."

"Yeah, give them the mystery meat." Jerome grinned, choosing a sword. "Maybe they'll give us some pork. Plus, it's past time for the kitchen to butcher some chickens."

"They're still laying eggs." Ezra frowned. "Don't be ungrateful. You aren't starving."

"Speak for yourself."

I chuckled and headed for the main entrance to take stock of our supplies. It was always better to have more than we thought we'd need. Experience had taught me to be prepared for anything. The new city looked to be at least a three-day hike, maybe more.

What if we were tied up and couldn't return as soon as we thought? What if one of us was injured preventing that person from travel for a day or two? The possibility of things that could go wrong was endless.

I'd make sure someone detained Jerome before we set out. I wasn't going to risk his young life for the unknown.

2

I pushed open the door hidden by the Ferris wheel which had fallen to ruin way before my time. It now loomed above our compound. I stepped into a darkness broken only by the gas fires burning in the distance. Fires that had burned since the destruction of the world.

The odor of decay and oil permeated my nostrils. Despite the doom and gloom, it felt good to be above ground.

After a few minutes of listening for signs of roaming malignants or soldiers and finding nothing to alarm me, I stepped onto the broken concrete. "Coast is clear."

Fawke joined me first, then the others. "Lars?"

"Crynn is right. Coast is clear for the next two blocks. Go left."

I turned in that direction. My boots crunched across what once had been the grounds of a popular amusement park. Now, the tunnels beneath had become our home. Sometimes the place felt more like a prison than a haven.

"Nice to be outside." Fawke flashed a smile.

"It is. Maybe we need to patrol more for our own well-being."

"The more we leave the compound, the easier it is for Soriah to find us. We are much wanted people, you and I."

I smirked. "Let them come."

"We aren't ready." Always the coolheaded one, Fawke strode forward to take the lead.

When I'd first arrived outside the walls of Soriah, I'd been the leader of a small group destined to remain there for ten years or until death—a fate bestowed by the spin of a wheel. When we'd learned that Soriah meant for us to clear the city in order to expand, we chose to rebel, no longer allowing ourselves to be ruled. Over time, more rebels joined us until we numbered in the hundreds. Unfortunately, that number wasn't all fighters. We didn't have near enough people prepared to start a war.

In the distance a malignant shrieked. The hair on the back of my neck rose. I pulled my sword from its scabbard. If those things heard or smelled us, they'd be on us in minutes.

Fawke motioned for us to move slowly and quietly, then pulled his weapon. Holding it at the ready, he continued forward.

"Stop." Lars' command came through the earpieces. "Three critters at ten o'clock and moving your way. Another two a little farther out straight ahead. You'll have to fight them after the first three."

"How long?"

"Less than fi…wait. They've stopped. Something behind them caught their interest. The second two are now heading toward the first three. Looks like they're going to go in the opposite direction."

Good. If they didn't know we were there, we might make it till morning unscathed.

"If they come around again, I'll try to draw them off with a drone. Out." Lars went silent.

We continued our tour, staying as close to the shadows as possible with a moon flitting in and out of the clouds. The occasional shriek of a malignant would halt us. Lars would give the all clear,- and we'd move forward again.

Hard to believe a year had passed since I'd spun that wheel. I glanced over at Fawke. If he hadn't rebelled along with me, he'd be gone from here next year. Did he regret his decision?

He peered at me, his gaze warm. "What?" He mouthed.

I shook my head, not wanting him to know my foolish thoughts. Being eight years my senior, he'd most likely think my thoughts childish despite his love for me. The last thing I wanted was to be considered childish. This world didn't allow those actions.

Lars broke into my thoughts. "Two o'clock. Coming from a two-story building."

I glanced over to see two malignants slowly emerge from a building. They lifted their snouts and sniffed the air. Hard to believe the hairless beings with large foreheads, beady eyes, and large fangs had once been human. Long legs and arms helped them gallop across the ground with great speed. They'd been human before bombs filled with poison fell on the city. Poison that warped their DNA.

The occasional rainfall still held traces of poison keeping both human and malignant undercover during the rain. Thankfully, the rain didn't contain enough of the warping agent to do much more than sear the skin.

I gripped my sword as the two malignants swiveled their heads toward our group. We formed our fighting circle of packs in the middle as we stood back-to-back.

The monsters shrieked and sprinted toward us. One thing the morphing of their DNA hadn't given them was intelligence.

With a primal yell, Fawke and I stepped forward as one, our swords effectively decapitating the malignants. More shrieks rose in the distance.

"Lars?" My eyes tried to penetrate the night.

"You need to find shelter. Fast. Three minutes and you'll be surrounded. Head for the building those two came out of. Heat sensors don't show signs of life."

We didn't need to be told twice. Snatching our packs, we darted for the protection of the building. I prayed we weren't walking into a trap. Not that I didn't trust Lars. I did with my life, but mistakes happened.

I halted the group just inside the door and listened. No shrieks of monsters, no cries of humans. To my right rose an iron staircase a bit twisted from the partial collapse of a nearby wall, but it looked sturdy enough to take our weight. I glanced back and pointed.

Without question, the others followed on my heels, still regarding me as the leader the cursed wheel had made me. It had heaved a great responsibility on my young shoulders—one I'd often prayed would be lifted. All I'd managed to do was coerced Fawke to share the burden.

The stairs shook under my feet but held. I entered a cavernous room with concrete pillars and shattered windows. Dropping my pack against a wall, I pasted myself near a window and gazed upon the dark city.

A group of about twenty malignants approached, stopping now and then to sniff the air. They avoided the gas fires, clinging to the shadows as much as possible. When they turned away from the building where we hid, I joined the others.

"A cold meal tonight." Kira gave an apologetic smile. "Can't risk a fire."

"It'll be a cold night, too." I pulled my coat tighter and accepted the strip of dried meat she held out to me.

Fawke handed me a canteen. "We'll share. If we have to keep hiding, our supplies might not last until we return to the compound."

"Let's hope we don't have to keep hiding. Thanks." I took one big swallow and handed the canteen back. Biting into the meager meal, I grimaced. I did miss the meals my mother had prepared behind the walls of Soriah. Fresh vegetables, fresh meat, and clean water back then. But that was before fire and death had made everything reek of decay. I had to tell myself freedom would make the sacrifices worth all the discomfort.

After relieving the hunger pains in my belly, I reclined against my pack and closed my eyes promising to relieve Dante of watch duty in an hour. Thankfully, with all of us, we only had to stay awake for an hour each.

I woke to Fawke shaking me. "Time already?"

"No. We have company. Soldiers." He put a finger to his lips.

I bolted upright. The rest of the group already stood on guard at the top of the stairs. I grabbed my sword and joined them.

Gunfire and shouts erupted, filling the bottom floor of the building. The staircase shook as feet pounded upward.

"They're bringing the monsters straight to us." Ezra shook his head. "We ought to shoot them as they come."

"No. We never kill unless we have to." I stepped forward. "We always have to see whether they'll join us first. It's the best way to increase our numbers."

As the soldiers appeared at the top of the stairs, our group moved back. Their eyes widened, but they wasted no time on us. Instead, they turned and fired down the stairwell, taking out the first wave of malignants.

I held my sword at the ready in case any slid past them. Fawke leaned over the railing and joined his gunfire with that of the soldiers. "Done." Fawke stepped back and trained his gun on the soldiers. "Weapons down. Kick them over here."

When the rest of my group trained our guns on the soldiers, they dropped and kicked them. Hands went up.

The soldier who had reached the top of the stairs first glanced from Fawke to me. "We've been looking for you guys for months."

"You found us." I pressed the tip of my sword to his throat. "Now what? You going to try and take us in?"

"That's what we're supposed to do."

"But?"

"The five of us broke away from our larger group. We heard you take in deserters."

I glanced at Fawke who shrugged.

"That will be hard to prove."

"Not really. They're bound to have heard the gunfire. They'll be coming. Once they do, they'll start shooting at us first, then you." His hands started to drop.

I pressed the sword tip harder against his throat. We'd have to leave before the rest arrived, but what to do with these five? "Moses, take over here, please." I motioned my head for Fawke to join me a few feet away. Dante quickly took his place.

"What do we do?"

He glanced at Dante who stood at the window. "See anything?"

"Not yet…hold on. Yeah. A tank and about ten soldiers headed this way. Lars, get us out of here."

"I'm working on it. Keep your pants on."

"What do we do with these men?" I glanced back. "I don't want to kill them; nor do I want to let them go free to follow us." Normally, we blindfolded them, took them back to the compound, and locked them up until we decided. A luxury we didn't have this time.

"If you leave us, they'll kill us," the soldier said. "We don't know this city like you do. We're newly arrived."

I sighed. "Since we confiscated all their weapons, we could take them with us."

Fawke nodded. "Okay. We'll search them first then hightail it out of here." He gave the order for Moses and Ezra to search the men and take their weapons. Then, keeping them in the middle of us so we could keep an eye on them, we descended the stairs, climbing over the bodies of dead malignants. Already the stench of rotting meat made it hard to breathe.

"Okay." Lars came back online. "Turn right after leaving the building. Go three blocks, then turn right again. Continue straight. In about a mile, you'll come to a field of tall grass. You have to go through it to reach the city."

My blood chilled. The smarter malignants hid in the tall grass knowing they could leap on us before we saw them.

We'd be walking through a gauntlet of razor-sharp teeth and claws.

Chapter Three

The grass didn't move in a night with no breeze. Rising like thin silver swords in the moonlight then inky when clouds covered the sky. My mouth dried and my palms sweated.

"I guess I should tell you our names." The soldier I'd been talking to stepped to the side of me.

"Why?"

"Because some of us aren't going to make it across that…" He waved his arm. "I'd like for you to dispose of our bodies while knowing our names."

"Fine." I couldn't take my eyes off the danger in front of us, despite Fawke's presence on my left.

"I'm Rick. That's Owen, Luke, Major, and the big guy is Hank, but we call him Tank."

"I'm Crynn and this is Fawke." I rattled off the names of the rest of our group before facing Fawke. "Do we have a plan?"

"First we give the soldiers back their guns." He shrugged. "We're going to need all the firepower we can muster. After that…I'm still thinking." He motioned for Ezra and Moses to give the men back their weapons. He returned his stare to the field in front of us. "I know it's harder to move, but those who have riot gear, wear it. Those who don't, stay behind those who do." He took a deep breath and squared his shoulders. "This isn't going to be pretty, but if we're quiet, we might get lucky."

Being quiet, moving through the grass undetected was our only chance and a very slim one at that. "I think we should wait until sunlight. The malignants are less active in the daylight."

"I agree." He glanced at the sky. "But the heavy cloud cover is not in our favor. I'll take first watch."

"If I can sleep, wake me next." I plopped next to my pack and stretched out. Time for silence and prayer. I closed my eyes to the sounds of the others readying to catch some sleep. The rustle of packs being lowered, and the whispers of conversation laced with fear.

Fawke woke me two hours later. "It's all quiet."

I reached for my canteen and nodded. "Let's pray it stays that way." I took a drink and pushed to my feet, grabbing my sword on the way to the edge of the field.

The clouds overhead thickened. A small breeze played with the grass. Both things would make it harder to detect something in the field besides us. I glanced over my shoulder in the direction of our compound. While I couldn't see the Ferris wheel, I knew it was there, and everything in me wanted to run back to the protection of the compound. Instinct told me only evil lay ahead of us.

I caught the watchful gaze of Fawke, his eyes glittering until the moon once again hid. For the first time in a long time, his presence failed to calm me. Having him there only increased my anxiety. People were going to die. Was it selfish to pray it wasn't him?

The sun rose earlier than I was ready for, rest time short because of the travel we'd already done. I glanced overhead at the darkening clouds. We didn't have enough gear to protect us all if it should rain. Unless the soldiers had protective gear, they'd be at the mercy of the poison rain. The only good thing was that the malignants would not be out.

I moved among the group, quietly telling everyone to prepare for rain. Luckily, the soldiers had rain gear.

Once we were ready, we formed a tight group. I took the first step into the grass. My heart leaped to my throat, subsiding when no monster lunged at my throat. Fawke stepped next to me and waved the others forward.

The only sound was the rustle of our feet as we moved as silently as possible, stopping every few yards to listen and watch for grass moving against the breeze. When none came, we continued. The field seemed to stretch for miles.

"You'll most likely not clear the grass till nightfall." Lars' subdued tone echoed in my earpiece. "So far, I don't see any threats coming your way. I'll send the drone out farther. If I find anything, I'll try to lure them away."

I tapped my earpiece, the signal that I'd heard

without confirming with words. There would be no unnecessary talking until we were clear of the field, which wouldn't be for hours according to Lars.

"Hold up," Lars said. "Weird movement ahead."

I raised my fist for the others to halt.

"Whatever it was stopped. You're good to go."

I glanced at Fawke, his features set in hard lines, then followed him forward again. That cursed wheel might have designated me as leader, but there were times when I was more than happy to let his expertise take the lead.

A shriek sounded to my right seconds before Lars told us to freeze again. My breath came in fast gasps. While I wasn't afraid to fight, I liked knowing where the attack would come from.

"There is definite movement," Lars said, "but I can't pick up an actual visual on the drone. They're staying below the top of the grass."

Skulking and slithering along the ground. "Should we make a run for it?" I whispered.

"Not yet. Keep moving slow and quiet."

My heart threatened to beat free. I wanted Lars to tell us to run back the way we'd come. To forget the quest of finding the strangers the drone had discovered.

Fawke reached over and put a hand on my arm. He smiled behind his mask. My nerves settled a bit as they always did at his touch.

One of the soldiers behind us tripped and let out a loud curse.

We all froze.

Several shrieks rose, closer this time.

I glared over my shoulder.

The man, Luke or something, gave a sheepish grin. "Sorry."

A malignant leaped from the tall grass, sinking its teeth into Luke's shoulder.

I pulled my sword as another pounced. "Where are you, Lars?"

"I'm here. I didn't see them coming."

"How many?" I swung, severing the creature's arm. Black blood splattered my mask.

"Maybe fifteen or twenty. Hard to tell until they jump out."

Great. Another swing decapitated the monster in front of me. I whipped around to meet another.

Shouts and the clash of swords filled the air. The malignants were too close to shoot leaving us in a battle of hand-to-hand combat.

Sweat trickled down my spine under the riot vest I wore. A malignant tried biting my shoulder only to meet material it couldn't penetrate. I grabbed a dagger from my belt and thrust it up under the creature's ribcage. Hot blood coated my hand. A rancid odor assaulted my nostrils.

I shoved the monster away and turned to the next one, stepping back until my back almost touched Fawke.

The rest of the group fought the same way except for the soldiers who swung both punches and bayonets like untrained baboons.

Kira yelled and shoved one of the soldiers away when his bayonet reached a little too close to her ribcage.

I shook my head and turned my attention to the

one wanting to tear my throat out. By the time the last malignant fell, my arms ached, and my legs trembled. Too much time in the compound had left me weak. "Are we good, Lars?"

"For now."

I glanced at the drone hovering overhead. "You can keep searching instead of hanging around here."

"Yes, boss." The drone darted away.

"How many wounded, Kira?" I wiped my sword clean and returned it to its scabbard.

"One soldier dead—Luke, the first one that got attacked, and two injured. One bitten and one cut by friendly fire." She stood over the bitten soldier. "Anecdote or bullet?"

"Anecdote, please!" Owen held out a pleading hand. "You need all the fighters you can get, right?"

"How much did you bring?" Fawke asked.

"Seven doses." She glared down at the wounded soldier. "If I give one to him, that is one less for us. Plus, we have to find a place to hide out for at least twenty-four hours. Make up your mind, though, because the longer we wait for me to administer it, the longer we have to hold up."

I gave an inward groan. "Give it to him." I knew firsthand the pain and fear that went along with being bitten. "Lars, we need a place to spend some time."

"On it."

I watched as Kira administered the shot before moving to stitch up Major. The man's wound didn't look too serious. A minor gash to his ribcage. Hopefully, it wouldn't keep him from holding his own during the next fight I knew would come.

"Okay. It's still going to take you a few hours, but if you turn right and keep going in that direction, you'll come across an old metal building, a shed of some kind, that should suffice for the night if it isn't a nest for monsters. So far, I don't see any."

"Thanks." I motioned to the others. "Let's go. Rick, your men can help Owen. We can't wait for you."

"Understood. We'll find you."

I hoped so. Owen was right. We needed every available fighter we could find.

I nodded. The rest of us took off at a jog, trusting Lars that the coast was clear. If not, we'd clear the way for the injured behind us.

The decision now was whether to leave the soldiers to recuperate in the shed while we paid a visit to the new city, or wait and take them with us. Something Fawke and I could discuss during our time of rest...and waiting.

There. Rising above the grass sat a rusty metal shed. No door and no coverings on the windows, but the roof looked to be intact. It would suffice for now.

Fawke and I entered first, scouring the place. The foul odor inside and nests of dried grass told us we'd most likely found the home of the malignants we'd killed. If it wasn't theirs, then the occupants would return. We'd dispose of them then. In the meantime, the odor was the best protection against the creatures we could ask for.

I dropped my pack against the far wall and peeled off my riot suit and leather coverings. Cool air caressed my skin, and I gave a sigh of relief, shaking my hair free of the helmet I wore.

A mewling drew me to the farthest nest. With my heart in my throat, I glanced down. "Fawke."

He joined me and muttered a soft curse.

Staring up at us with blinking red eyes common to the albino-colored malignants was an infant monster.

Chapter Four

Then, we found another and another hiding among the straw nests.

"What the hell are we supposed to do with those?" Ezra peered over my shoulder. "I say we kill them before their mommies come back."

"I think we killed their mothers." I glanced at Fawke. "Idea?"

He chuckled. "We can't keep them as pets. Before long, they'll realize we're food. But we don't need to decide now."

Could I kill a baby anything? Yes, they'd be lethal soon. Yes, we were sent here to rid this place of the monsters, but they were still innocents and not so very far off from humans, genetically speaking. I shook my head and plopped down next to my pack.

Maybe we could study them…stupid idea. What would we do with them while visiting the new city? Besides, I'd be risking those in the compound by taking back malignants.

Fawke sat next to me. Since we'd stood guard the few hours before daylight, it was up to the others to keep watch for a while. "What are you thinking?"

"Stupid things." I leaned my head back. "I can't kill them."

"Let Ezra do it." He laughed again.

"This is serious." I narrowed my eyes.

"Is it? We are in a metal shed with three baby monsters. We most likely killed their parents already. They won't survive anyway." He turned to face me. "I don't mean to be callous, only realistic."

"I know." I sighed.

He entwined his fingers with mine. "We're going to succeed, Crynn. We're going to gain freedom back for the people."

"Will we?"

"Absolutely. Have faith."

"A lot of people will die."

"They're willing to take the risk. They're all willing to follow you."

That's what scared me the most. It turned out I had a gift for leadership, but with that gift came great responsibility. "I'm glad you're here with me."

He raised my hand to his lips. "Me, too."

Commotion outside had both of us on our feet and reaching for our weapons.

"It's the soldiers," Gage said. "I don't see anything else."

Kira directed them to put the injured men against the far wall away from the infant malignants. "No need to tempt the beasts."

"What in the world?" Rick jumped back when one of them hissed.

"Don't worry. I'm going to dispose of them once Crynn gives the order. Right now, they help disguise our scent." Ezra flashed a grin, clearly looking forward to preventing the three infants from maturing. As the oldest in our group and a lifetimer for having committed murder a long time ago, Ezra had far more experience than I ever hoped to attain.

"How long until he's ready for travel?" I glanced at Kira.

"Hopefully by morning." She placed the back of her hand against his forehead. "If there's no infection by then, he'll be good to go."

"Lars, some scouting, please." I pressed my earpiece.

"Got it."

"Try to determine whether those in the city are friendly and where the entrance is. I remember seeing walls." I sat back against my pack.

"Will do."

"You're anticipating them not being friendly." Dante sat across from me and Fawke.

"Just in case." I forced a smile. "I find it strange that we've not seen or heard from those living a few days' hike away."

"Maybe they never leave. Maybe they have everything they need within the walls of their city." He shrugged. "I wouldn't leave the compound if I didn't have to. We're gambling with our lives every time we leave there."

We were. I closed my eyes, hoping to get some rest if only my mind would stop spinning with what ifs. What if we didn't kill the infants? What if those in the new city were unfriendly? What if we never took down Soriah?

I must have fallen asleep because I woke to Lars' voice in my ear.

"Ten-foot wall around the place. Massive wooden gate. A deep moat surrounding a city that looks to be several acres large. The moat is filled with water. There's an oily substance floating across the surface. These people don't intend to allow anything, or anyone, in without approval."

I frowned. "How would they have been able to build a moat without being attacked by malignants? It had to have taken days, weeks, or maybe longer."

"The military?" Rick offered. "You think you came before the army, but you didn't. Soldiers have been out here fighting for years. The outskirts mostly. Only recently have they gone into the burning cities."

Why had I not known this? From the look on the rest of my group's faces, they hadn't either. "This could be part of Soriah trying to repopulate outside its walls." Which meant we could be walking into a trap.

"Should we keep going?" Kira glanced up from where she sorted supplies.

"We could take a vote." Moses' dark, serious eyes darted from me to Fawke.

"I'll take the drone in closer," Lars said. "See what I can find out. I'll let you know if I find weapons, or if they shoot the drone down. If not, maybe those behind the walls are friendly. You guys stay put until I report back."

"We're not going anywhere until morning." It wasn't wise to visit strangers during the night. Dark was for ambush and traveling undetected—not an appropriate time for what I hoped would be a friendly visit.

Rain fell, continuing through the rest of the day and into the night. The group cleaned their weapons to fill the time, occasionally casting furtive glances to where the infants now huddled together in one nest.

The babies were growing hungry, and their shrieks increased.

"If we don't shut them up, they'll call every malignant within earshot." Ezra reached for his sword and shot me a quick look.

I nodded, averting my eyes. When I turned back, straw covered their little bodies to shield them from my sight. I sighed and stood in the doorway of the shed as the rain continued to fall.

The clouds overhead looked a little less black. Maybe over time, the poison would be washed from the sky, and rain would no longer burn holes in our skin. I'd read in a book about people dancing in the rain. What would that be like? What would it be like to dance in the sunlight without a care? Would I ever see such a time?

I shook off my dark thoughts. If not for the hope of such things as dancing in the sunlight, why prepare for a war we might not win? All we had keeping us going was hope.

The rain stopped by morning, and Lars once again spoke into our earpieces.

"I didn't see any weapons, but I can't see into buildings. They have livestock and gardens. Not many folks were walking around, and the few I did see hid when the drone flew over."

"So, you can't tell us how many reside there?" I frowned.

"No, sorry. Also, the way there looks clear. You should be arriving within a few hours. Be careful leaving the grass. The moat pretty much starts where the grass ends."

"You heard him, folks. Pack up. We're moving out." Fawkes hefted his backpack to his shoulder. "We move as quickly and silently as possible. There could be more malignants in the grass."

A certainty, but we might make it through unnoticed if luck chose to be on our side. With a glance at Fawke, who nodded, I stepped outside, grateful for the leather suit I wore to protect against the raindrops balancing on the stalks of grass.

The wet ground muffled our steps, the only sound the rustle as we moved forward. No breeze blew. We'd see anything coming by the movement. Maybe luck was on our side.

In the distance rose a wall of logs reaching for the sky like sharp fingers. Again, I wondered how something so massive could've been built without attacks from malignants. Maybe they had been attacked but simply disposed of the threat. Perhaps soldiers had protected the builders long enough.

"Impressive," Fawke said softly.

"Intimidating." I flashed a smile. "Would you rather live above ground or under?"

"I'll wait and see what that place has to offer, but I'm happy wherever you are."

My heart warmed as his words drove away all the maudlin thoughts in my head. I didn't need luck.

With Fawke Newton at my side and faithful friends at my back, I had everything I needed.

I stepped from the grass and stood inches from a moat full of inky water. If Lars hadn't warned us, I might have stepped forward too far and taken a deathly plunge.

A heavy wooden door towered over us. To the right of it rose a drawbridge. The door didn't open, and the bridge didn't lower as we gathered together.

"It isn't as if we can knock," Gage said. "How do you expect them to know we're here?"

"I'm pretty sure they know." I craned my neck to see the top of the wall.

No one stared down at us. From the other side came the frenzied barking of a dog. A dog? I grinned at the normalcy of something I hadn't heard since leaving Soriah.

My smile faded as the drawbridge started to lower.

Chapter Five

I pulled my sword and waited to see whether we'd be greeted by friend or foe while the others crowded closer to me. Old habits of protecting the leader were hard to overcome, I guess.

A man in clean tan pants and matching tunic stepped onto the drawbridge. Behind him stood five men armed with simple rifles—the kind people used to hunt with a very long time ago.

"Those guns would barely slow us down." Dante stepped closer to my left side.

"Hopefully, we won't have to find out." I squared my shoulders and waited as the man in tan approached.

A wide smile spread across his face. "Welcome to Peace." He held out his arms. "We weren't aware there was anyone else out there besides the army."

"We've been here for a long time." Fawke held out his hand. "I'm Fawke Newton. This is Crynn Dayholt." He introduced the others. "We're simply a scouting mission to find and exterminate the malignants." He motioned his head toward the towering walls. "Impressive."

"Call me Governor. Everyone does." He returned Fawke's handshake. "Please, come in and rest yourself." He tossed me a sharp look as if he somehow knew who we were and that I was the leader, not Fawke. The curl of his upper lip told me he didn't approve.

So, I took a step behind Fawke, more than happy to take second place.

The governor led us through the gate and the drawbridge immediately started to rise.

My gut told me to run back the way we'd come, and I exchanged a wary look with Fawke. The same wariness crossed his eyes. With the massive gate and towering walls, we had no easy way out.

The governor glanced over his shoulder, his smile still in place. "I can have food and drink brought in. You look tired and famished." He opened a simple wooden door and ushered us into a long room containing a table and about twenty chairs. "This is my committee room—the place where we make our plans to keep Peace running smoothly. After we eat, I'll show you around. During the meal, you can tell me more about yourself." He motioned for Fawke to sit, then nodded at the rest of us.

"I do hope you plan on staying for a few days. Rest up, put on some clean clothes—" He tilted his head. "I'm assuming you are the ones behind the drone we saw a while back?"

"We've found it to be the best way to scout large landmasses." Fawke removed his sheath and set his sword on the floor at his feet.

I did the same, still doing little more than taking in our surroundings.

Ezra leaned close. "You letting Fawke take the lead on this one?"

"Yes. Something feels off." I kept my features impassive and my gaze on the governor. Stupid title. I wanted to know his real name.

Two young men brought in platters of food. Ham, potatoes, carrots, and freshly baked rolls. How big was this place that they could keep a large supply of fresh vegetables?

As if reading my mind, Governor chuckled. "All your questions will be answered momentarily, Miss Dayholt."

"How long has this city been here, Mr., uh, Governor?" I lifted my plate for one of the servers to fill.

His brow furrowed. "I do believe it's been about twenty years. Time tends to get away from a person out here." He folded his hands on the tabletop. "We're an experiment, you see. A rather successful one, if I do say so myself."

"Explain." Fawke bit into a roll.

I did the same almost moaning out loud at the fresh, yeasty taste.

The governor shrugged. "Soriah is wanting to take back the country, one city at a time. Since those monsters are too numerous, we built this place. Once those walls went up, we had no need to leave. It's people like you that help keep this place safe. I'm assuming you're Stalkers?"

"With a few soldiers tossed in." Fawke stabbed

a fork into a hunk of ham. "Others have had something similar to this in the mountains until malignants pushed them out."

"Where are you staying now?"

Fawke simply smiled. "I'm curious to see what is different in Peace than what those on the mountain had."

"Besides the protection of these walls?" The governor arched a brow. "Eat. Rest. I'll show you in due time." His gaze flicked back to me, then at the food in front of him.

This man knew exactly who I was. I glanced in the corners for cameras or a monitor, something that let him communicate with Soriah. Once my group and I had decided to rebel against the white city, I left the monitor turned off that allowed us to speak to Sharon, the president's right hand.

The governor snapped his fingers, then waved one of the servers over. "Make sure two cabins are readied, one for the women, one for the men. Have clean clothes left for them." He smiled back at us. "You've come such a long way, surely you'll stay a night or two."

It wasn't as if we had much choice unless we wanted to scale the wall.

"That's generous of you." Fawke reached under the table and squeezed my hand. "We're glad to accept your hospitality as long as the two cabins are right next to each other."

The governor nodded. "Of course. Why should you automatically assume I can be trusted? I feel the same way about your group."

"You said this place is an experiment?" I set my

fork on the edge of my plate, my stomach fuller than it had been in over a year.

"I came here with a group of people twenty years ago and a plan drawn up by Soriah. A large number of soldiers accompanied us and helped us build this place. We are very happy here. Things run like clockwork. If you're finished with your meal, I'll show you."

Chairs scraped against the wood floor as we stood. I felt awful about not finishing the meal set before me, but not being used to such generous portions, I could only hold so much. I picked up my scabbard and followed Fawke and the governor outside.

Buildings lined a dirt-packed street. A covered walkway connected each of the buildings. A clever way to move around even during the rain.

I didn't see a single woman or child during our tour, not even when the governor showed us the massive greenhouse that held the vegetables.

"We have a large barn and several pens that house our chickens, hogs, and a few deer we raise for meat." He pointed to a large building at the end of the street. "Most of what you see are homes, but a few work buildings are scattered here and there. A clothing shop, a kitchen, a butcher, a woodworking shop—everything Peace needs to function." His chest puffed out.

"Where are the women and children?" Fawke's eyes darted from building to building.

"They won't be allowed to meet you until I know you can be trusted. Our women and children are our greatest asset." He set off toward the barn.

"You'll be pleased to know we even have milk cows."

I really wanted to know how we could get our hands on some of the milk, produce, and meat other than rats. But our compound had nothing to trade other than weapons and ammunition, neither of which I'd willingly give up—not with the war against Soriah looming on the horizon.

Any hopes of recruiting help from this place dissipated. People happy with their circumstances did not usually want to shake things up.

We stepped into a massive building filled with the odor of manure and the noise of livestock. These people had thought of everything when building this place. They'd taken into account the rain and the fact that their population would grow.

"Do you have medical personnel, Governor?" I asked. "Someone to care for the people and the animals?"

"We have everything we need, Miss Dayholt." The governor led us down the middle of the barn to where a sow lay under several wiggling piglets. "We are completely self-sustainable."

"Fresh water?"

"That was a bit trickier, but we possessed the means to sterilize what falls from the sky. We're also built over an underground creek. Rest assured, we have everything we need."

The man started to sound repetitive, almost as if he felt he needed to convince us that they did indeed have everything they needed.

"And, what we may not have, we can obtain with the right persuasion." His gaze darkened as it landed on me. "Soriah likes to trade. We get what we cannot grow or build ourselves by sending them fresh produce." His tone seemed to leave out something important. I had the feeling he would trade more than produce if it suited his purpose.

"Are there other cities like this?" Fawke petted the head of a fawn.

"While I haven't seen or heard of any, I'm sure there are. How can Soriah grow without new cities like this one?" His smile faded. "Not all of us want to rebel, Miss Dayholt, Mr. Newton."

Fawke's hand rested on the hilt of his sword. "So, you do know who we are. What do you plan to do with the information?"

Chapter Six

I woke to a silent apparition in gray standing next to the cot I'd slept on. I bolted to my feet. "Whoa."

"Good, you're awake. Do not be frightened. I am here to take you for your bath." The woman nodded to the clothes folded at the foot of my cot. "You and your friends. We've brought you something to wear while your other items are cleaned."

I glanced at Kira, who shrugged and picked up the clothes on her cot. "A bath sounds nice. It's been a while."

It really did sound nice, but I wasn't sure how much I could trust this woman in front of me. A long gown brushed the ground around her feet. A hood covered all of her head, and a thin piece of matching cloth covered her face. She must be sweltering under there.

"What's with the getup?" Gage frowned,

glancing at the pile of clean clothes in her hands. "At least these are tan and not gray. I can tell you right now, I'm not covering my face."

The woman said nothing and turned to lead us from the house. She stepped into another building with several wooden tubs lined up against one wall. Three other women stood with pitchers in hand. Obviously, we each would have our own attendant.

"Please. Choose your tub. I will return when you are finished to show you to the dining hall." With a nod of her head, she left us in the hands of the others.

I felt self-conscious as I peeled off my filthy clothes. This was the first time I could remember disrobing in front of strangers. Dropping the clothes in a pile on the floor, I stepped into a tub and stretched out. Immediately, one of the women poured hot water into the tepid bath. When she grabbed a bar of soap and a rag to wash me, I shook my head. "I can manage, thank you."

She dropped the soap into my hand and stepped a few feet away while the other women waited on Gage and Kira who didn't seem to mind someone else bathing her.

"Why not be pampered?" Gage grinned. "Doubt I'll enjoy this experience again."

As I scrubbed the filth from my skin and hair, I thought back on the night before. The governor had changed the subject when Fawke asked what he intended to do with the information of our arrival on his doorstep. Soriah would pay heavily for our heads. Is that what the governor had planned? To collect the bounty?

"What's your name?" I asked the woman holding a towel for me, narrowing my eyes to see through her veil.

"We have not been given permission to speak to you." Her words rose barely above a whisper.

"Oh." I raised my brows at Kira. Dressed from head to toe so I couldn't tell anything about the woman, and she was not allowed to speak? What kind of place was this? I noticed an embroidered number on her chest. Fifty-six. "Can people tell who is who by the numbers?"

She nodded.

"You have no real name?"

She gave a one-shouldered shrug.

Okay. She had a name but went by a number. Why? When she went through puberty? I shook my head and dried off before donning the thin cotton clothes waiting for me. How much did I really want to know about these people? A lot.

The first woman, number Seventy-Two, returned and motioned for us to follow her. A light drizzle fell from the sky, but the covering over the walkway kept us dry and free from the acid rain. When we arrived at the same building we'd eaten in the night before, Seventy-Two backed away, then turned and left us.

With a quick glance at Kira and Gage, I opened the door to see the rest of the group already seated. My eyes locked with Fawke's. His hard gaze softened a bit but didn't stop the muscle ticking in his jaw. Something had happened that he didn't like.

I took my seat next to him and reached for his hand under the table. He gave me a quick squeeze before pulling free.

Okay.

"You look much better, Miss Dayholt." The governor smiled.

"The bath was wonderful, thank you, Governor." I tilted my head. "May I ask a question?"

"Absolutely." His expression darkened.

"Why are the women here dressed from head-to-toe in gray and given numbers instead of names?" I pasted a smile on my face and did my best to seem merely curious.

He rolled his head on his shoulders, then folded his hands on the table, spearing me with his eyes. "We arrived here twenty years ago with a set of rules and regulations from President Crane. Things he hoped would improve the way Soriah was run. One of those regulations was a woman's role in our new society." His smile widened. "Once they reach womanhood, they are given a number, dressed modestly, and married off. Their sole purpose is to reproduce and wait on the hardworking men of Peace. The role suits the women well. They are very happy."

My blood boiled. "How do you know? Have you asked them?" No woman could be happy under such circumstances.

"What a bunch of bull." Gage slapped the table. "In our group, women are equal. Crynn is our leader and one of our strongest fighters other than Fawke."

The governor's brows rose. "And since you women are not fighting, you are not bearing children. You will die out. Peace, on the other hand, is flourishing."

I shot Gage a warning look to keep her from saying anything else. I didn't want the governor knowing we had our own community. "Where are the children?"

"Kept out of sight and educated."

"The girls, too?" I arched a brow.

"Until they are of marriageable age, yes." The man truly didn't see the wrong in how he led his people. "Miss Dayholt, we have no crime here. Everyone knows their place and is happy to remain in it. Can you tell me that you do not have the occasional dissension among your ranks?"

"No, I cannot, but we work it out as a group."

"And no one has a problem being led by a mere slip of a girl?"

"She's far tougher than she looks." Fawke stiffened. "I'm sure you're aware of the wheel in Soriah. You know how careers are chosen."

He nodded. "We have something similar for our men here. It's a system that works. How unfortunate for you that Miss Dayholt spun the wheel and landed on leader of the Stalkers. Had it been a male that spun the wheel, perhaps your group wouldn't be…on the run."

"On the contrary, Governor, it was fortunate for us that she landed on the black square. Crynn is a natural leader." Fawke stopped talking when two women in gray brought out the food and placed it in the center of the table.

Now that we'd seen them, there didn't seem to be any reason for their appearance to be kept secret. "Thank you," I said.

So, my assumption was right. The governor did

know exactly who we were. All that remained now was to wait and see what he had planned.

"Do not speak to the women, please. You will distract them from their work." The governor speared his fork at a piece of—was that bacon?

My mouth watered. I hadn't had bacon since leaving Soriah. "My apologies." I had to restrain myself from grabbing a handful.

The governor's eyes sparkled as if he could read my mind. With a snap of his fingers, a woman in gray set another platter of bacon in the middle of the table.

I flashed a grin and took a few more pieces.

"You're quite an attractive woman, Miss Dayholt. A pity you're a Stalker. You should be married and bearing children."

"Someday, she'll marry me." Fawke smiled my way.

Marriage? Really? I might like that. Until landing on the black square after spinning the wheel, marriage and a family was all I'd dreamed about. Fate had changed that.

"Ah, when things settle down." The governor steepled his fingers. "What if they don't settle down, Mr. Newton?"

"Then we'll figure something else out."

"I see." He nodded, seeming pleased. "Miss Dayholt might have landed on the black square, but it is clear to see who the true leader of this group is. Well done for keeping some semblance of gender roles in place. The best you can, anyway."

I frowned, holding back a retort. At Fawke's look, I ducked my head and concentrated on my meal. It didn't hurt anything to let the governor think Fawke was the leader. He assumed the role every bit as much as I did. In fact, I'd offered it to him at one point.

"I've planned something special for you today." The governor puffed out his chest. "A wedding. This is a prime opportunity for you to witness our life in full detail."

Oh, goody. Nothing I'd like more than to see a child wed. No one had to tell me it wouldn't be a girl barely out of puberty.

"We have a feast afterward. It's a grand time." The governor finally started to eat. "Everyone comes."

"Thank you for the invitation." Fawke picked up his fork. "We'd be honored to attend."

"Your women will need to wear gowns. They cannot move around the city in trousers." His tone left no room for argument.

"As long as it isn't gray, I'm good," Gage muttered.

I kicked her under the table. With some of the "kindness" leaving the governor's words the more he spoke to us, the less we needed to voice our opinions. At least for now. We didn't need to cause trouble. Enough trouble was coming without asking for it. I cleared my throat and reached for the wooden cup of water next to my plate. It held a slightly bitter taste, and I grimaced.

A satisfied gleam shone in the governor's eyes as I set my cup down. I narrowed my eyes as my mind grew fuzzy. "You drugged our water, Governor? "He shrugged. "We need to make sure you are docile enough to attend the wedding. I assure you no harm has been done."

"Drugging someone without their knowledge is harm enough." I dipped my fingers in Fawke's water and patted my forehead in a desperate attempt to clear my mind.

Gage and Kira's features had settled into a benign expression, their eyes vacant, a slight smile on their lips. The men stared with wide eyes at our host.

Fawke glared at the man. "Do you plan on turning us in to Soriah?"

"I haven't decided yet, but a lot of it will depend on you. Two of your women are of childbearing age."

Chapter Seven

I tossed out that Kira was a great healer and more than a baby producer, then excused myself from the table. As soon as I stepped outside, a woman in gray moved to my side. Obviously, walking around the city unescorted was a big no-no.

Heaving a sigh, I glanced up and down the dirt street with absolutely no idea of where to go. What building was off limits? I wanted to see the school and the infirmary, the kitchen…I longed to see how these people lived. Were they as happy as the governor stated? I didn't see how they could be.

Doing my best to ignore number Eighty-Six next to me, I crossed the street having decided to look in every building I passed. Curiosity might have killed the cat decades ago, but that very thing might help me figure out what to do about the governor. He didn't seem likely to let us leave. Especially not after having mentioned knowing about the bounty.

The first building I peered into seemed to be a

modest home. Since the few windows held no glass, with only a piece of fabric over the opening, seeing inside was easy.

A double bed with a trundle, hooks on the walls for clothes, a washbasin…nothing else. The home was a bedroom. My eyes cut to the woman next to me. She probably lived in such a home—a place designed for one thing only. Making babies.

I glanced in several more identical places before reaching the place we'd bathed, and there was nothing but tubs in there now. Next door to the dining hall was the kitchen. Iron pots hung over fires. Wooden tables provided workspace. Women moved about like silent wraiths preparing the wedding feast.

Soriah had every modern convenience known to man. Why hadn't these people brought some with them instead of living so far back in time with nary a book to describe modern life elsewhere?

I continued until I found the building used as the school. Maybe thirty children, all dressed in clothes made of the same tan material as I wore, sat on benches with long tables in front of them. On the table sat tablets and chalk. At the front of the room stood a woman in gray. Seeing her as a child would have frightened me away from education. To these children, seeing the woman fully covered was an everyday thing. How could they pick their mother out from the others?

"Crynn."

I turned to see Fawke strolling toward me.

"I've been sent to inform you that it is time for you to put on a gown." He grinned.

"Yes, master." I laughed, shooting Eighty-Six

a quick look. The woman stood as silent as a statue. "I'm here to do your bidding."

"As if." He gave me a quick one-armed hug before stepping away. "No sense in shocking our hosts with public displays of affection." He lowered his voice. "What would they think?"

"That I, being the lowly woman, should be stoned." I gave him a quick kiss. "See you at the wedding."

"I'm not wearing this." Gage pointed at a pile of gray garments on her cot as soon as I entered our room.

I frowned. "I'm not crazy about them either. Let's wear everything except the veil. We don't want to cause too many problems."

"When are we leaving this place?" Gage yanked off her shirt and tossed it on the cot.

"As soon as Fawke finds a way. We can't exactly scale the walls." I quickly donned the surprisingly soft gown and headpiece. At least we wouldn't be uncomfortable.

"Where did you go?" Kira wrapped the headpiece around her head.

"To get a better feel for the lives of these people. Remember the history books of old? Way back in the 1800s and before? They live like that. No running water, no electricity, and other than the bedrooms, they all use the community buildings. I didn't see where the single women and men sleep, but I didn't have time to look at every building." I smoothed the gown over my hips. "Let's make the best of things until Fawke finds us a way out of here."

"What if he decides he likes it here?" Gage

shuddered.

"He won't."

"We were drugged at breakfast. What if our men are brainwashed? It could happen."

"Again, let's not borrow trouble." Fawke was too strong to fall for such trickery, right? "If the men do fall into the governor's trap, then it will be up to us to save them. And ourselves. A united front, ladies?"

"Absolutely." Kira grinned and held out her hand.

We held hands, forming a line of three, and stepped from the building. Eighty-Six hadn't moved. She turned toward us, but the veil kept me from reading her expression. Imagine what she and the other women could do if they united?

Outside, we fell into step with the residents of Peace flocking toward the end of the street. The women outnumbered the men three to one, and most of them seemed to be pregnant.

"The men must have more than one wife," Gage whispered.

"The fastest way to reproduce when there are more women than men." Kira glanced behind us. "I don't see a single man who looks over the age of sixty, and it's hard to determine the age of the women."

"Old women can't bear children." My blood chilled. "Where are their elderly?"

Eighty-Six hissed and held a finger to her lips. She shook her head and motioned her arm to where the women of Peace had gathered on one side of a makeshift aisle. Men stood on the other side. Once the governor, dressed all in white, stood at the front, everyone sat on the stools provided.

A man who appeared to be in his thirties moved to the front. A few seconds later, a woman dressed all in gray glided down the aisle. When she reached the man, the governor linked their wrists.

"Today, this woman is joined to this man's family. She has become his fourth wife and will from this day forward be known as Ninety-Two. Her birth name is to be used no more."

The men stomped their feet while the women remained silent.

The happy couple faced the leader who placed a hand on each of their heads. "May you have a productive life together."

"I feel like gagging," Gage whispered.

"Shh." While I felt the same, it wouldn't do to draw attention to ourselves. We were already receiving way too many glances from the men. I shot one a stern look, and he turned away. When I faced forward again, my gaze clashed with the governor's.

High spots of color appeared on the man's cheeks. His eyes flashed. Keeping his smile in place, he announced that the bride and groom would lead the way to the feast. "Miss Dayholt, please accompany me."

My mouth dried. I nodded and fell into step beside him.

"Smile, please." When I did, he continued. "I cannot have my men casting lecherous looks at you and the other two women. I must ask that you wear the face cloth."

"If we don't?"

"I will be more inclined to turn you over to Soriah. Keep smiling." He waved as we passed a couple of men watching. "If your group will conform to our way of life, we could use you here."

"And Kira?" The older woman didn't have many childbearing years left. Not like Gage and I did.

"She will work in the infirmary until she is no longer useful. I have several men interested in wedding Miss Blue."

"And then what?" When I stopped, he pushed me forward. "Don't touch me."

"My dear Miss Dayholt. I could give you a wonderful life here. My wives live in luxury, such as we have. You would no longer have to fight. No longer be something other than what a woman should be. You would be happier in your role as a woman."

I rolled my eyes and searched the crowd for Fawke. Finding him casting a wary eye at us, I relaxed a bit. "I have the man I want to spend the rest of my life with."

"Mr. Newton is admirable for sure, but he does not keep you in your proper role. By not doing so, he risks your life. Women are far too valuable." He placed a hand on the small of my back and ushered me into the dining hall. "Please consider my offer, Miss Dayholt. It will not come again."

When he stepped away, it occurred to me that he hadn't answered my question as to what would happen to Kira when she was no longer deemed useful. I sat in an empty chair, releasing a shaky breath when Fawke sat next to me.

"You okay?" He asked softly.

"You'd better watch out." My smile trembled. "The governor just proposed to me."

He arched a brow. "Really? Should I challenge him to a duel?" His lips twitched.

"It isn't funny. Things are getting serious very quickly. Several men have expressed an interest in Gage."

"I'd like to see them approach her." He chuckled. "On a more serious note, the governor has asked that I convince you and the others to cover your faces."

"How will you tell us apart without a number? Only married women get numbers."

"I don't know how that works, but if you are blending in, you can go places I can't. You can see and hear things I can't. We really need to start thinking of a way out of this place. I doubt we'll find any converts here."

He was right. I gazed down the very long table. Only men, our group, and the wedding couple sat. The women stood against the walls, plates in hand after the rest of us had been served. I liked being treated as Fawke's equal. His partner. Not even a life of so-called peace could convince me to live the life these women did. I'd rather fight malignants every day.

As if my thoughts had conjured them, a shriek sounded on the other side of the wall, followed by another and another. I sprang to my feet, reaching for the sword I didn't carry. The rest of my group did the same.

"Sit, please. No need to be alarmed." The governor waved his hands. "Those monsters cannot reach us here. Other than Soriah, this is the safest place in the country."

I slowly lowered myself back to my seat but couldn't resist casting a look toward the wall. Malignants had sharp claws. What if they learned to scale the wall? If they figured out a way across the moat, scaling would be easy. I whispered my concerns to Fawke.

He nodded. "I've thought the same myself." He raised his voice so the governor could hear. "We've been discussing the possibility of the malignants finding a way across the moat."

Murmurs rose around the table.

Again, the governor raised his hands. "That is impossible. They would have to build a structure."

"Or find something to use." I leaned forward to peer around Fawke. "History shows that even the apes learned to problem solve."

He laughed, soon to be joined by most of the men around the table. "Fantasy, Miss Dayholt. This is why women should not possess too much education. They are unable to distinguish fact from fiction."

"Sir, the malignants are evolving." Fawke's features hardened. "We've seen it. They were once human, remember? The more they associate with us, the more they learn. I would use caution if I were you and not discount their intelligence."

"Can you defend this city if they come over?" Ezra shook his head. "I don't see a fighter among you."

"If you are all so worried about something that will never happen, stay and guard our city." The governor tilted his head. "Or…train some of my men to do so."

Fawke glanced at me. When I nodded, he turned his attention back to our host. "We can train your men."

The governor turned a stony gaze on me. He didn't seem to like the fact Fawke didn't make the decision to train men without asking me. "Very well. We begin tomorrow. You can start with sticks, then progress to your weapons which we have kept safe for you." A slight smile teased at his lips. "We can't have you using real weapons against my men, can we? Not until I can fully trust you."

Chapter Eight

Yet another apparition in gray stood next to my cot when I opened my eyes the next morning. "I need my regular clothes," I mumbled. "No argument. I can't train fighters in a dress. Feel free to tell the governor I forced you to comply." I swung my legs over the side and sat up, rubbing the sleep from my eyes.

"My clothes, too." Gage sat up.

"I'm good since I've been ordered to go to the infirmary." Kira stood. "I might as well look the part."

I wanted to tell them the governor wasn't lord over us, but I kept my mouth closed. As long as we resided within these walls and ate the food of Peace, we had no choice but to go where we were told…most of the time.

When I arrived at the morning meal in my "regular" clothes, I earned a glare from the governor. "I can't train the men in a dress." I felt like a bird that constantly repeated itself.

"I naturally thought Fawke would do the training."

I arched a brow and waited for Fawke to respond.

"Crynn is as good or better of a fighter than I am. She's won against men twice her size in hand-to-hand combat. Along with the rest of our group, we'll all train your men." Not leaving room for the other man to argue, Fawke dug into his eggs.

Eggs! And more bacon. The food alone almost tempted me to want to stay. We had eggs on occasion but not nearly enough for the amount of people in the compound, and we never had bacon.

"My men will be too distracted to learn." The governor scowled.

"When I smack them across the rear end with my stick, they'll pay attention." I flashed him a grin before digging into my breakfast. The opportunity to spar always filled me with joy. Even more so when I used my skills for teaching. I hoped I wouldn't be teaching men who would someday face us in a battlefield.

"I've ordered a space in the center of town to be cleared and used as a training area. You'll have every man aged sixteen and older."

"No women?" Gage glanced up from her food.

"Surely not."

She shrugged and returned to eating. "Since the women outnumber the men in this place, it makes sense to train them."

"I disagree, and this subject is closed."

I nudged Gage under the table with my foot and

gave a slight shake of my head. If she antagonized the man too much, he might lock us up. Then, we'd never find a way out of here. I glanced through the open door at the wall. If we did find a way to escape, we still had the moat to deal with.

"Ready?" Fawke pushed back his chair and rose to his feet.

"Yep." I stood and smiled. "I'm always ready."

He laughed. "Yes, you are."

The governor didn't join in our repartee. His features remained set in stone as he stood. Back ramrod straight, he led us from the building to where the dirt street had been packed as hard as rock.

At least thirty men from teens to forties awaited us. Near them sat a barrel full of sticks as thick as a man's forearm. I stood and waited, letting Fawke take charge. The men would be more trusting with him taking the lead. I had to constantly remind myself that these were not my people.

"Gentlemen, grab a stick and form a line in front of each of these people." Fawke motioned to our group. Minus the soldiers who had accompanied us, there were seven of us ready to train these men. The governor sat in a chair ready to watch the proceedings.

Kira, dressed all in gray, tossed us a wave, put her face cloth in place, and headed to the infirmary. Several of the men's gazes followed her. The governor might be wrong as to whether some of them wanted her as a wife.

The line in front of me and Gage was a lot shorter than the ones in front of the men. Fawke frowned. "First, let me show you what you'll be learning. Crynn?"

Grinning, I grabbed a stick more than ready to show these men what I could do. I held the stick at the ready and waited.

Fawke lunged forward. I raised my stick to ward him off. A loud crack filled the air. We danced apart, both watching for the other one to make a move.

We clashed, we danced, we grunted, we grinned. Tossing Fawke a wink, I kicked out with my right leg and swept his legs out from under him. He landed on his back with an oomph, then jumped to his feet.

"Not fair." He wagged his finger at me and lowered his stick, then faced the watching crowd. "As you can see, the women are skilled enough to train you. Let's form those lines again."

Some of the men, mostly the younger ones, shifted to either my line or Gage's. Fine by me. The fewer men in my line, the more training they got.

I glanced at the governor. "Care for a try?"

He waved a hand in dismissal. "I know how to fight, Miss Dayholt, as do some of the older men. Please proceed."

The first young man in line stood unmoving, his eyes wide. I whirled and whacked him on the backside. "Get your stick up. If I were a malignant, you'd be dead."

He raised his stick waist-high.

"Higher." I hit him again, this time in the gut. "Fight!"

"I can't hit a woman."

"I'm not a woman right now; I'm a monster." I

screamed and lunged.

The boy raised his stick in front of his face and cowered.

I swung my wooden sword, stopping just short of his neck. "You're dead. Again." I hit him harder this time, and again and again until a spark of anger shone in his eyes. Good. "Hit me. Stop acting like a little girl." That did it.

He roared and lunged, swinging his stick at my head. I deflected and whipped around, pleased when he blocked my swing. After a few more minutes, I stopped and grinned.

"Very good. Take a rest. We'll go again later."

I taunted and teased each man who stood in front of me until they grew angry enough to fight. Perspiration ran down my back and face. My breath came in pants.

"Next time, we use real swords." Fawke tossed his stick back in the barrel. "See you all here tomorrow morning. Good job, gentlemen."

"I'm ready for a bath." My grin stayed glued on my face. "That was fun."

My smile faded when the largest man I'd ever seen emerged from one of the houses. He moved behind the governor's chair and crossed his massive arms.

The hair on the back of my neck rose as his dark gaze followed me to the bathing house. Frigid fingers skipped up my spine. Did the governor have a personal bodyguard? After witnessing my group's skill at fighting, did he feel threatened?

A woman in gray scurried past me and into the building. "I'm so sorry the water isn't ready."

"It's fine. I didn't ask for a bath before now." I sat on a stool and stared through the open door. The governor and his giant stared in my direction.

"Creepy." Gage rushed inside. "See that man? I'm glad he wasn't in my line."

"He wasn't in mine either. He just now came out of a house."

She froze. "What does that mean?"

"I have no idea, but it's not good."

Another woman in gray entered with two full buckets of water. She handed one to the other woman and they started filling the tubs.

"I really want to go home." Gage shed her clothes and stepped into a tub. "The water's cold."

"The women aren't finished filling it." My gaze remained locked on the governor's.

Since he refused to look away, I pulled the curtain from the hook holding it back and let it fall across the door before I disrobed. Then, I lowered myself into the tub and requested a bit more hot water. My muscles would be screaming by morning.

Once the water had reached the temperature I wanted, I scooted down as far as I could without submerging my face and closed my eyes, letting the heat take some of the stiffness from my limbs and back.

"I'll see you later."

I made a noise of acknowledgement as Gage dressed but kept my eyes closed. "More hot water, please."

The snapping of fingers popped my eyes open.

The governor held a pitcher of hot water and waved a hand for the woman tending me to leave. He slowly poured the water into the tub while I glanced around for something to cover myself.

"Don't trouble yourself, Miss Dayholt. I've seen many women's bodies."

"You have no business seeing mine." I crossed my arms across my chest. "What do you want?"

He pulled up a stool and sat down. "That was quite the exhibition outside."

"Nothing more than what we were supposed to do." I leaned up far enough to reach the towel on the floor. Not caring about it getting wet, I draped it over me.

"It's commendable how someone who acts so unlike a woman can still be so modest."

"Why?" I frowned. "You expect me to act like a man and wander around naked? Curse? Pee standing up?"

He laughed. "There's the crudeness I expected." His smile faded. "Do you know what my men are doing right now?"

"Nope, and I don't care."

"They're gambling for your hand and that of Miss Blue's. Gambling, Miss Dayholt."

"What a waste of time." I rolled my eyes wishing he would leave. Where was Fawke? He rarely let me out of his sight.

"The arrival of you and your group has disrupted the peace of my small city." His eyes flashed. "I seriously suggest you reconsider my proposition and your place here." He planted his hands on his thighs and pushed to his feet.

Fawke barged through the curtain and skid to a halt. He glanced at me, then glowered at the governor. "What is going on here? How dare you come in while she is bathing? What would you do if one of your men did the same?"

"I make the rules here, Fawke. I can do as I please." He held up his hands. "Relax. We were simply having a conversation. As you can see, Miss Dayholt is covered by a towel."

Because I grabbed one. I narrowed my eyes.

Fawke's hands curled into fists. "It's improper for you to be in here."

"Worried about her reputation?" The governor tilted his head.

"Maybe." Fawke stiffened.

"Do not fear. If anyone says anything derogatory, I'll simply marry Miss Dayholt, which will stop the rumors. It's far worse for both of us to be in here than just me. My people trust me. You, on the other hand…" He smiled at Fawke, then at me, then strolled from the building.

I climbed from the tub, wrapping the soaked towel around me. "I want out of here, Fawke. There's something very, very wrong here. If we don't leave, he's going to find a way to force me to marry him." A fate far worse than death.

He stepped forward, taking my hands in his. "I won't let that happen. I'm working on a way out. I am. This place is a fortress. We may have to dig our way out. But I have a plan before we resort to that. Whatever you hear about me, play along."

Chapter Nine

Gage stormed into the building as I tugged on my boots. "Have you heard?"

"Heard what?" Boots on, I stood and reached for my top.

She planted her fists on her hips. "Fawke was overheard talking to the governor about possibly converting to his way of thinking." She lowered her voice and leaned closer. "And…there's a monitor here. I saw it myself. More than one actually. You know what that means. And…there's no training today. The men are too sore."

"Soriah most likely knows we're here, and the men of Peace are weak." I hadn't turned on the monitor in the compound for months. I didn't want Sharon, the president's right hand, to know our every move.

"What about Fawke?"

"I'm sure he has a reason for saying that." This must be the plan he spoke about yesterday. "*If* he said it." How did he expect me to play along if he didn't tell me his plan?

Kira joined us, her arms full of gray clothing. "Fawke said you're to wear this. The governor won't allow you to leave this building unless you do."

"See?" Gage pointed at the clothes. "Fawke has lost his ever-loving mind." Tears sprang to her eyes. "He's betrayed us."

"No, he hasn't. He's trying to get us out of here. Go along with it."

"What if you're wrong?"

"Then God help us." If it was true, I'd have to find a way out of here myself and leave with a shattered heart. I disrobed and donned the gray articles of clothing. As I fastened the face cloth over my face, I closed my eyes to gain some composure. When I opened them, they fell on the embroidery over my left breast. Visitor One.

"Ugh. I'm number two. Kira is three."

"Be glad your number isn't higher. That would mean you're married." I laughed.

A split second later, they joined me until the three of us were almost hysterical. I fought to regain my breath. "That felt good." Maybe things weren't as dire as they seemed. "Show me the monitor."

"Okay, but we'll have to be sneaky. It's kind of hidden."

I started to ask how she'd found it, but decided I didn't want to know. The important thing was we knew something we weren't supposed to know. That gave us a little power.

"Follow me." Gage ducked outside.

"I need to get back to the infirmary. Let me

know what you find out." Kira stepped outside.

When I joined Gage, Kira was gone. "Don't rush. We don't want to attract attention." At least the face covering would keep Sharon from recognizing me. Still, if I could help it, we'd turn on the monitors without being seen.

Halfway down the "main" street, Kira led me between two buildings to a shack set off from the others. The route had no covering against the rain. The shack looked more like a storage shed than anything. As we approached, a voice drifted through an open window.

We ducked, pressing our backs against the wall.

I slowly stood and peered through the window. The governor sat in front of a desk with several monitors. On one he spoke to a man I'd never seen before. The others showed different streets of Soriah.

On every street strolled women dressed all in gray. I slid to a sitting position. "Soriah is now just like this place." I explained what I'd seen.

Eyes wide, Gage shook her head. "Who's the man?"

"I have no idea, but I'm going to assume he's taken Sharon's place. If women have a lower status, she wouldn't be President Crane's right hand anymore." I stood to peer inside again.

"Are you sure this woman and her group are no longer a threat?" The man in the monitor narrowed his eyes. "President Crane will want you to hold them until he can send soldiers to apprehend them."

"Yes. The male, Fawke Newton, is coming around. If he does, the others will follow. If not, we'll dispose of those who don't. Never fear. President Crane has nothing to worry about."

I widened my eyes. The president would never stand for that. He'd flaunt my body in Soriahas an example for anyone considering rebellion.

The man in the monitor shook his head. "No, they must come here if they refuse to conform to our new ways."

The governor gave a heavy sigh. "Very well. If they do come around, I may take Miss Dayholt as a wife, if Newton will let her go. She'll be well subdued at that time and no longer a threat to Soriah."

I'd like to see him try. My hand clenched so hard my fingernails dug into my palms.

"Our new way of life is successful," the man said. "We cannot allow a group of rebels to ruin that. Find out how many there are and where they are hiding."

The governor nodded. "I will do my best."

"That's not what I'm saying. I'm telling you to do it. Gain the confidence of this man named Fawke. Drug him, brainwash him—whatever it takes. If not him, choose another. Just get it done." The monitor went dark.

The governor ran his hands through his inky hair, then pushed to his feet.

I ducked back down, shoving Gage toward the back of the building.

The sound of the door closing told us he'd gone. After several minutes of not hearing him return, I scooted to the front door. Locked. We'd have to gain access through the window. Why lock the door when none of the windows closed? I shook my head.

"You'll have to lift me up. I want to see more of what's going on in Soriah. Once I'm inside, be my lookout. Give me enough notice to get out."

"I'll try." She knelt down and cupped her hands.

I stepped into them. As she lifted me, I grabbed the window frame and struggled to pull my leg up and over. Not easy in a dress.

"Good thing you're small." She gave me a toss, sending me through the window.

I landed in a heap on the floor. Dust flew up through the cracks. I sneezed and froze. When no shout of alarm came, I stood and approached the monitors.

Except for the dress of the women, nothing seemed different, other than the fact there seemed to be fewer women on the sidewalks. No children and no one with gray hair.

My blood ran cold. What had Soriah done with the elderly?

I fell into the only chair. No one had arrived to be a Stalker after me. Had they done away with the wheel? I needed to find out what was happening here and there. The question was how?

"Incoming." Kira's harsh whisper came through the window.

I bolted to my feet and dove out the window. The impact with the ground took my breath away. Kira hauled me to my feet and dragged me gasping behind the building.

Footsteps passed. After a few minutes of me

regaining my breath, we slipped back onto the road and made our way slowly to the infirmary. Instead of entering, I turned toward the wall.

"Let's walk along it and see if we can spot a place of weakness."

"What if they catch us?"

I shrugged. "We're simply out for a stroll because we have nothing else to occupy our time. I want to study the lookout platforms a bit."

"If we're caught, we'll be assigned to some horrible job for sure."

"We'll worry about that when and if the time comes." Without being too obvious, I studied the wall as we passed. The only way out was over or under. If we were to dig a hole, they'd spot us. We couldn't dig one from our room. It was too far away. I turned and studied the line of buildings. The closest to the wall were the single men's quarters—a place we wouldn't be allowed to enter under any circumstance. Hopefully, Fawke and the rest of our group could find a way to dig undetected.

Speaking of, Fawke marched toward us, a slight smile on his face.

"How did you know it was us?" I tilted my head, lifting my face covering.

"Who else would be on an idle morning walk?" He lowered my covering.

Gage crossed her arms. "I heard about you talking to the governor."

"Good. I wanted the news to get back to Crynn. It's the only way I could think of to earn us a little more freedom. I did tell Crynn to play along."

"Yes, you did." I filled him in on what I'd

found on the monitors. "Things are getting bad. Tell me you're digging a hole."

He laughed. "Under my cot. I hope we find another way, because digging is going to take a very long time, and eventually someone is going to notice the dirt piles behind the houses."

"He plans on drugging and brainwashing you." I gripped his arm.

"I'm on the alert. I don't drink anything unless it's from the same urn his drink is from. I don't eat anything unless he eats it." He put his hands on my shoulders. "The governor won't catch me unaware, Crynn. I promise." He cut a glance toward Gage. "And I won't be turning to the other side. Neither will any of the rest of the group. You're going to have to trust us."

She lifted her chin. "Okay."

"The governor says training will resume in the morning. He's adamant the two of you not participate this time."

I rolled my eyes. "Don't tell me. We're a distraction."

"Yes. We have to go along with his orders for as long as possible. I need for him to trust me. Especially since Soriah wants your head on a stake. We're safe as long as we're in compliance. When the time is right, we'll make our move."

"Coming here was a bad idea. No one here will join our cause unless it's the women, and none of them will be fit for battle." Hopefully, if we did escape and some came with us, we'd have time to train them before war started.

On the other side of the wall, a malignant

shrieked. Scratching on the wall raised goose bumps on my arms. "Are they trying to scratch their way through?" I gasped. "Fawke, they've crossed the moat."

Chapter Ten

Fawke shoved me toward the dining hall. "Find the governor. I'm gathering our weapons."

"What if they won't let you have them?"

"They will. Go." He sprinted away from me.

Hiking my dress to my knees, I yelled for Gage. We darted to the place I hoped the governor held court. The city needed to act fast before the malignants breached the wall. How had they crossed the moat?

We burst into the dining hall. The governor was not there.

"Where is he?" I headed toward two women setting the table for the noon meal.

"In his cabin." One of them shrank back.

"Where. Is. That?"

"The last one on the right before reaching the wall. The larger one." She scurried from the building, leaving the other woman frozen on the other side of the table.

Most likely, they weren't used to two women barging in and demanding to know where their leader was, but desperate circumstances demanded desperate measures. I motioned my head to Gage, and we took off at a sprint in the direction of the last building on our right.

My heart leaped into my throat to hear more shrieks and scratching. Did the governor not hear them? His cabin almost touched the wall. Should those things get in, his home would be the first place they went.

His cabin was the only one with a door instead of a curtain. Even his windows had shutters.

I raised my fist and pounded. Within seconds, a woman in gray, her face clear of its covering, answered the door and stepped back, averting her face. Number Eighty-Six was a lovely redhead with a smattering of freckles, hazel eyes, and didn't look to be more than sixteen or seventeen. I glared at the governor who sat in a large wooden chair. Lecherous old man.

"The malignants have crossed the moat." I crossed my arms. "Aren't you the least bit concerned?"

"What concerns me is how you feel you have the right to barge into my private residence." He stood, his face set in hard lines. "The two of you have much to learn about proper comportment for a woman. Fawke or one of the other men should have come to me."

"They're busy gathering weapons and, I hope, fighters."

"Don't worry yourself, Miss Dayholt. The

monsters cannot scale the wall."

"They found a way across the moat."

"Yes, but you give them too much credit. When the bombs fell, those unfortunate creatures lost the ability to reason as we do." He exhaled heavily. "Follow me." He strode to the door.

"You're the one who underestimates them, sir. We've noticed firsthand how they are evolving." I had to rush to keep up with him, something I'm sure he did on purpose. The man would do anything to teach me my place.

He motioned a man over, then whispered something in his ear.

The other man paled, then nodded and rushed off.

"Up here, ladies. You'll have a good view of how we take care of the few monsters that manage to penetrate the wall." He bowed at the ladder leading to the platform.

"Crynn." Fawke tossed me my sword, then glanced at the governor as if daring him to take it from me. "You'll need us to be armed if they breach the wall."

"They won't." He pasted on a smile that didn't reach his eyes. "Come. See for yourself. This isn't the first time one of them has gotten lucky."

Climbing the ladder in a long dress and carrying a sword wasn't easy, but I managed. At the top, I lifted my face covering to allow a breeze to dry the perspiration from my brow before peering over the top of the wall to the ground which seemed very far away.

Two malignants looked up and screeched.

They dug harder at the wall with their sharp claws. I shuddered at the hatred in their eyes.

Across the moat lay a long wooden plank. They had solved a problem set before them. If they could do that, they'd soon find a way over the top.

"I told you they were learning to problem solve." I ripped off my face covering. As my breathing increased, the fabric was suffocating me. I stuffed it into a hidden pocket of my gown. "Your people are no match for them."

"Watch and learn, my dear Miss Dayholt."

The massive gate opened, and a man in tattered, soiled clothing staggered out. In his right hand, he held a torch. With his wide eyes, he glanced to where the malignants dug at the wall. He tossed the torch into the moat.

With a whoosh, flames shot up, burning the makeshift bridge. The man darted back to the gate and pounded on it with his fists. "Let me in."

"Who is that?" My heart lodged in my throat as the malignants stopped their scratching and turned, lured by the man's pleas.

"One who refuses to comply. We keep them in a cell and use them as needed. This one had been sentenced to death for defiling a woman. He's received his just punishment." The governor shrugged. "At the same time, he helps the very ones he hurt."

"This is barbaric!" My mouth fell open. "Prisoner or not, this man is human."

His screams pierced my ears. My stomach rolled. The man's cries stopped, and I turned away as the monsters ate their prey.

"Now what? Those things are still on this side of the moat."

"Never fear, Miss Dayholt. Help is coming." He pointed across the moat.

The tall grasses on the other side bent as something came toward us. If that was a herd of malignants, we were in grave danger. My group and I could handle ten malignants, but a herd? Impossible. We'd all be slaughtered.

"Soldiers." Gage spoke in a hushed whisper. "How did they get here so fast?"

I narrowed my eyes at the governor. "Mind answering that question?"

He chuckled. "They're here in case I have to turn you over to them. Instead, we'll use them to dispose of those two. At least for now." His threat hung heavy in the air.

Soon, heavy gunfire made hearing anything else impossible. Bullets riddled the two malignants and pocked the thick wall of Peace. One of the soldiers tossed the governor a salute, then led his men back into the grass.

I lifted my worried gaze to Fawke. If looks could kill, the governor would be a pile of smoldering ashes. Instead, he gave the ghost of a smile. "Thank you for believing us worthy of your city instead of a prison cell."

"Soriah is trying to repopulate this world. Young people are valuable." His hard gaze landed on me. "Too valuable to dispose of lightly. Come. The noon meal should be ready."

"Think I've lost my appetite for a week," Gage muttered, descending the ladder.

The rest of our group waited at the bottom. "What happened?" Ezra stepped forward.

"The soldiers disposed of the malignants." Fawke watched as the governor continued ahead of us. "The governor sacrificed one of his prisoners."

"I'd like to know where they keep them." I glanced up and down the street. "I didn't see anything that looked like a jail when Gage and I were walking along the wall."

"Keep looking." Fawke pressed his hand on the small of my back. "There are more things going on in this city than we're aware of."

Which scared me more than being thrust on the other side of the gate with malignants. The unknown always frightened me the most.

Chapter Eleven

Before we reached the dining hall, men swarmed around us and removed our weapons. My grip tightened on the hilt for a second, before I reluctantly allowed them to take my sword.

Scowling, I marched into the hall and took my seat. I pulled my face covering from my pocket and set it next to my plate before meeting the governor's glare with a sharp one of my own. The placing of the face covering was to let him know I'd comply with his rules. For now.

He nodded and snapped his fingers for the meal to be served, then looked past me to Fawke. "I'm sure you understand now what happens to those who don't follow the rules."

"You sacrifice them to the malignants." Fawke crossed his arms. "It doesn't take a genius to see that, but no, I don't understand. You sent a man to a brutal death."

The governor shrugged. "One more thing. I

don't allow is women to come knocking on my door. If needed, one of my men can fetch me." He placed a napkin in his lap. "There was no time for my wife to prepare to welcome them or cover her face. I trust it won't happen again."

"I'll make sure of it." Fawke patted my hand under the table.

I understood he said what he needed to say in order to appease our host, but the constant reminders that women were considered to be lesser than men rankled me. I stared at my lap to conceal my thoughts and emotions. After the meal, I'd pretend to go to my room to lie down, but I actually planned to find the prison and discover what this town was hiding. It couldn't be just a place to repopulate.

A plate containing a chicken leg and vegetables appeared in front of me. I had to admit that as much as I hated the city of Peace, I would miss the food. We had chickens and a garden, but not nearly enough to feed our people on a regular basis. Instead, we doled out fresh meat and vegetables in rotation, unless we were heading out on a mission. Then, we ate well whether it was our turn or not. I couldn't help but wonder whether these people appreciated the food despite the rigidness of their lives.

When I'd finished, I excused myself saying I had a headache and asked Gage to accompany me back to our house. The governor recommended a visit to the infirmary, but I waved him off.

"A short nap will suffice, thank you." I nodded and rushed from the building.

"Do you really feel ill, or is this a ploy?" Gage put her face covering in place.

I did the same. "A ploy. Come on. I want to find out where they house the prisoners." And anything else the governor might be hiding.

Folding my hands piously in front of me as I'd seen the other women do, I fought to keep my pace slow so we didn't draw attention to ourselves. I also wanted to take another peek at the monitors in the outlying shed. Right now, that was our only way of ascertaining what Soriah was up to. We weren't going to win the war without information.

It troubled me so much had changed since the last time I'd spoken to Sharon. I veered to the left and quickened my pace until Gage and I reached the shed. A peek inside showed it empty. Once again, she hefted me up.

The monitors showed me nothing new. Armed soldiers on street corners. Women in gray heading down the sidewalks. No sign of any children. While I couldn't see what the women looked like behind their head coverings, I didn't see any men over the age of fifty. Soriah was a larger version of Peace.

I joined Gage outside. "Nothing more than what I saw the last time."

"Are you looking for a way in?"

I shook my head. "My mother told me a few months back that she knows of a tunnel we can use to get into the city when we're ready to strike. One that has been boarded up but should still be useable." We might not have enough fighters yet, but plans to attack Soriah were moving ahead.

A new worry tickled my mind. "Let's visit Kira at the infirmary." She'd been working long hours, coming in after I'd gone to bed and leaving before I woke. If I did see her at mealtime, she rushed off after eating.

Kira and one other woman were tending to a woman and a young boy. When Kira spotted us and I moved my face covering aside so she could tell it was me, she joined us in an adjoining room. "Are you two okay? Anyone else sick?" Worry flickered across her eyes. Medical personnel weren't required to cover their entire face, it seemed.

"We're fine." I glanced over her shoulder to make sure no one listened. "What's the matter with those two?"

"The woman is in the early stages of pregnancy. The child has a cold." She frowned. "We rarely get anyone seriously ill."

"What happens if you do?"

"If they aren't improved in a few days, they…disappear."

My heart dropped. "Anyone die?"

"Not in here." She lowered her voice. "Something is very off, Crynn."

"That's what I'm thinking. What's the oldest patient you've had?"

"We had a man a little over fifty suffering chest pains. He was gone the next day."

"Dead?"

She shrugged. "Just gone. I asked the other nurses, but they acted scared and said they didn't know. I could tell they were lying, but I didn't press the issue. I don't want to disappear."

"Why would you think that?" My blood chilled.

"I may be a warrior, Crynn, but I'm past

childbearing years. In the eyes of Peace, I'm running out of usefulness."

We needed to find a way out and fast. I put a hand on her shoulder. "Nothing is going to happen to you. I won't let it. Trust me."

"With my life." She gave a short laugh. "You've pulled all of us out of tough times before."

I prayed I wouldn't let them down this time. After giving her a quick hug, I led Gage from the building. We had a jail cell to find.

"Maybe if we walk the perimeter of the fence?" Gage peered around us. "No one seems to be out and about with those heavy clouds overhead."

"It won't be pleasant if we're caught in the rain." Our clothes would protect us from a drizzle but not a downpour. I eyed the sky. We might be okay if we hurried. If not, we'd be making a run for an overhang.

"I'm willing to chance it," Gage said. "Fawke's way of getting us out of here is taking too long."

I agreed. Lifting my dress above my ankles, I dashed for the fence. No malignants screeched from the other side. How long until they tried to break in again? We'd be sitting ducks when that happened. There was only one way out, and that would require opening the gate and lowering the drawbridge.

We skirted the perimeter of the wall. I occasionally glanced toward the "houses," ready to study the sky if someone paid us attention. Thankfully, because of the impending weather, no one was foolish enough to be out other than me and Gage.

"Have you ever thought about what will

happen to our people if we don't make it out of here?"

Gage's words stopped me in my tracks. "Yes. Jenkins is capable of leading them. Nothing will change as far as the upcoming war against Soriah, except we won't be a part of it."

"You're the leader. The people need you."

A sigh emitted. I needed them as much as they needed me. The longer I stayed in this gray gown behind these walls, the less capable I felt at leading a rebellion. "Let's keep going."

"There." I leaned to study a part of the ground that looked different than the rest. Since our compound was under a fallen Ferris wheel of a long-abandoned amusement park, I recognized their attempt at camouflage.

A few pieces of discarded wood and planks lay haphazardly over a spot on the ground. If not for the nails holding them in place and the iron ring placed almost out of sight, I might not have noticed. I tossed Gage a grin and pulled up on the ring.

A trapdoor opened. A set of wooden stairs descended into darkness. On the wall past the second step hung a torch and a striker.

"Close the door." As she did, I lit the torch and led the way downward.

As we descended, I started to hear murmuring. My foot scuffed on a step. All noise ceased. We weren't alone.

The steps stopped at a well-packed dirt floor. Stretching on both sides of me were cells.

I swallowed against the nausea rising in my throat. The cells on the right held mostly men but a few women. The ones on the left held people with gray hair, and some appeared so weak they couldn't rise from their cots. Thankfully, I saw no children.

"Have you come to feed us?" A man gripped the bars of his cell. "Where's the food?"

"No, I'm sorry. We're…not…" I exhaled heavily. "Why are you here?"

"Because I am lame." He held up a foot wrapped in a dirty bandage. "I'm waiting to be disposed of. Those over there have committed crimes. They took a man away yesterday. Do you know what happened to him?"

I shot a look at Gage. Eyes wide, she shook her head.

"That man has been put outside the wall."

A grin spread across the old man's face. "We're set free when we leave our cell?"

I nodded, blinking back the tears burning my eyes. Death was a sort of freedom, wasn't it?

"Don't be daft." A man lying on a cot fell into a fit of coughing before continuing. "Do you really think this city has as many chickens as they eat? As many hogs?" He propped himself on one elbow. "Lady, they eat the old, the ill, those born deformed. Who are you that you don't know that? The man set free…the malignants got him. Correct me if I'm wrong."

I staggered back. Surely, he was wrong.

Gage gasped and clapped a hand over her mouth. "Crynn?"

"How do you know this, sir?" I stepped closer to the bars.

"Because I was once the governor's right hand

man until I took ill. After three days in the infirmary, it became obvious I wouldn't live. That gained me a home down here until the pantry runs low. Those poor fools across the aisle are monster bait, doomed to live down here until they're needed up there. A few days, a few months—it varies." He lifted a thin shoulder, then began another bout of violent coughing.

"Where's the key?" Gage surveyed the walls. "We have to free them."

"And let them go where?" I frowned. "Until we can find a way to escape, they have nowhere to go."

"The governor's wives have keys. They are the ones who feed us," the ill man said. "A spare key hangs on a hook near the front door of his house."

"Thank you." I nodded. "We are trying to find a way out of here. I promise I won't leave without you."

"Don't worry about me, young lady. Rescue the others if you can. My days are already numbered."

I wanted so much to help him. To find someone who could heal him of his ailment, despite the fact he'd once been as horrible as the governor in his beliefs. "If you're still breathing when the time comes, you'll be coming with us. I promise."

The trapdoor at the top of the stairs opened.

Chapter Twelve

Synchronized footsteps thundered toward us. I stepped in front of Gage, only to have her shove me out of the way. Since neither of us were armed, trying to protect each other served no purpose.

"Don't be a hero." Squaring my shoulders, I shot Gage a quick glare. "Do what they tell us. We need to live to fight another day." I transferred my gaze to the two men descending the stairs.

Both carried guns. One of them preceded the other one. "The governor has ordered you to be locked up until he determines your fate."

"Why?" Gage narrowed her eyes. "Because we discovered this place's dirty little secret?"

He grabbed her by the arm while the other man unlocked the cell. Once the door opened, he tossed her inside and reached for me.

I shook my head. "Touch me and I'll kill you myself." Head high, I strode into the cell and stood near an empty cot. Defiance in every line of my body, I tore off my head and face covering. Then, as the man still watched, I dropped my gown and grinned as he realized I'd worn my regular clothing under the dress. One more infraction against me, I assumed. "Well?" I waved my hand in dismissal. "Go on. Find out what our punishment is."

As one, the two men turned and marched back up the stairs.

What a bunch of pomp and circumstance just to lock up two women. I sighed and plopped onto the cot. How long until we knew what the governor planned? Would visitors be allowed down here?

Gage sat next to me. "I'm glad we had breakfast. I doubt we'll be fed for a while."

"We get one meager meal a day," an older woman said. "They want us alive but don't want to waste food on us. The meat is suspect, so I usually don't eat much."

My stomach roiled thinking of all the "chicken" I'd enjoyed. I fought to keep from losing my breakfast by taking deep breaths and staring at the one dim bulb dangling from the ceiling between the two rows of cells.

"Do you think we'll be executed?" Gage asked.

"I doubt it. We're too valuable for breeding. Whatever is planned won't be pleasant, though."

"If you're taken out of here," one of the men in the cell across from us said, "you won't be seen again. No one ever is."

Fawke wouldn't let that happen. Neither would any of those in my group. They'd fight for us.

No one came for us for hours. We had no food

or water, just mindless boredom and the raspy breathing of the ill. When the sound of the trapdoor up the stairs opened, Gage and I jumped to our feet.

The governor, flanked by the same two men as earlier, approached our cell. One of the men aimed a gun at Gage's head. "Miss Dayholt." The governor released a long sigh. "What are we going to do with you?"

When I didn't answer, he continued. "If it's a fighter you want to be, a fighter you shall."

I frowned. "I don't know what you mean by that comment."

"You will fight my best man, or Miss Blue dies."

Since I was very good with my sword, fighting anyone wasn't much of a challenge. "If I win?"

"You and your friends go free." His smile widened.

"Like the others you've locked up and released?" I arched a brow.

"No, as in you'll leave exactly as you came."

Somehow, I doubted that. If we weren't to be offered to malignants, the soldiers of Soriah would be waiting to arrest us. Still, this could be our only chance to escape this place. "Okay. When?"

"Now is as good a time as any." He stepped back and motioned for the door to be opened.

With my heart in my throat, I exited the cell and climbed the stairs. Flanked by the governor's men and Gage beside the governor, we headed to the area we'd used to train the men of Peace. I snorted at the town's name. This place was anything but.

It looked as if every resident was in attendance.

Our group stood separate, surrounded by men of the city. My blood chilled. This fight wasn't going to be what I expected.

I caught Fawke's gaze. Dread clouded his handsome features. My stomach dropped as I spotted the one I'd be fighting.

The massive man I'd seen with the governor entered the empty space in the center of the onlookers. I glanced around for my sword.

"This is hand-to-hand, Miss Dayholt." The smile faded from the governor's face. "You need to be put back where you belong—the weaker sex. Not on a level playing field, which a weapon would give you."

Five-foot-two-inches me against a mountain? I didn't stand a chance.

"This is insane." Fawke stepped forward, only to be held back by the governor's men. "He'll kill her. The man is three times her size."

"No, he will not kill her. But she will feel every strike." The governor nodded. "The fight will continue until she promises to conform to our rules."

Mountain Man was quicker than he looked. His first punch to my jaw knocked me sideways and dropped me to my knees. He gripped a handful of my hair and yanked me to my feet before shoving me away. I slid across the packed dirt, tasting grit and blood.

Stars floated in front of my eyes, and I struggled to my feet. I delivered a roundhouse kick to his ribcage that did nothing more than elicit a laugh from the man. Jumping out of reach, I balled my hands into fists as I tried to determine a weak spot. The eyes. I'd have to be quick.

I lunged, my fingers splayed. The man caught me midair and tossed me like a rag doll. I slid across the packed ground, the breath knocked from my lungs as I landed at the governor's feet.

He knelt, his gaze locking with mine, as I struggled to catch my breath. "Had enough? All you have to do is say 'I conform.' Say that Soriah knows best."

"And be…your…wife? Never." I staggered to my feet.

"Proceed." He waved a hand.

With a roar, Mountain Man thundered toward me. I leaped out of the way and whirled to meet his next punch. He struck me in the gut, again driving me to my knees. His next hit felt like it broke my jaw. The next my nose.

Blood spurted, covering the front of me. I knelt, my head hanging. Every breath sent shards of glass through me.

He grabbed my hair again and bent my head back, his fist ready to hit me again. I'd failed. Not even one good hit. The governor was right—I was no match for him.

"Stop!" Fawke raced to my side. "I pledge allegiance." He stood between me and Mountain Man. "I pledge my loyalty to the governor and the people of Peace and Soriah. I will make Crynn my bride and reside within these walls. Just stop this brutality."

Mountain Man grinned and clipped a solid hit to the side of Fawke's head, knocking him unconscious. Darkness clouded my vision before I fell over and gave in.

I woke in the medical building and stared into Kira's concerned gaze. "Where's Fawke?"

"They didn't bring him here. Don't talk." She handed me a glass with a straw, then a pill. "You're pretty beat up, Crynn. Take this. Rest is what you need."

"Not until I know what happened to Fawke." I tried to sit up and failed, my body too weak and battered. "What all is broken?"

"At least one rib, maybe more. Your nose. At first, I thought your jaw was broken, but it's back where it belongs." She patted my shoulder and leaned close to whisper. "I'll try to find out what happened to Fawke. Please stay in bed. The governor will put you back in the cell if he thinks you're capable of getting up."

"Gage?"

"Locked up along with everyone but me and you. I'll be back as soon as I can."

I nodded and closed my eyes.

When I opened them again, Kira stood over my bed. "Fawke is okay with nothing more than a headache. He's under guard in his cabin and fuming."

I laughed, then hissed against the pain in my ribcage. "That's good."

"Ah, Miss Crynn is awake." The governor entered the building.

Kira bowed her head, attached her face covering in place, and stepped back, eyes glittering with fury.

This stupid man had no idea of the fires he

stoked.

"You'll be a variety of colors come morning." He stared down at me. "I do hope the beating has taught you a lesson."

"Absolutely." Just not the lesson he wanted me to learn. What I'd learned was this man would die at my hands.

"Once you're up and out of bed, we'll have a wedding." He tilted his head. "I would've preferred you to be mine, but if Fawke sticks with his pledge, then…" He shrugged, then turned to Kira. "Send for me the instant she's able to get out of bed."

"Yes, Governor."

My gaze should've burned holes in his back as he left. Would my friends be released for the wedding? After? My mind raced. It became more imperative than ever that we find a way out of the city.

Not that I minded marrying Fawke, not at all. What I did mind was how heavy the guard detail would be until the governor was convinced Fawke and I would conform.

Kira gave me another pill, and I once again fell into a deep sleep.

I woke up with a start. Night had fallen. I turned to see a woman I didn't recognize dozing in a chair. Good. Kira was resting. Pushing to a sitting position, my breath caught at the pain. My mouth felt as if it was full of cotton. My stomach rumbled.

The woman's eyes popped open.

"Water, please."

She nodded and jumped to her feet. Seconds later, she helped me drink. "You were in the cells?"

"Yes."

"My father was taken there. He's ill. Did you see him? He would've been coughing."

"Yes." I sighed. "He isn't going to make it. I'm sorry."

Tears filled her eyes. "I know. I wish I could be with him at the end."

"I guess that isn't the way things are done here."

"I hate this place," she mumbled. Her eyes widened, and she stumbled back. "Forgive me. I shouldn't have said anything."

"Don't worry. I won't repeat what you said. Although I do have a question. Do you know a way out of here?"

"Only through the gate." She approached the bed again. "The lever to drop the gate is to the right. It looks like a simple plank." She gripped my hand. "Take me with you when you go."

"Are there others willing to leave?"

"Most definitely." Hope leaped into her eyes. "Mostly women and their children. Will you still take us?"

"I'll take as many as I can." The one thing the compound and Peace had in common was the realization that children were the future. Without them, mankind would not survive. "I'll let you know once a plan is in place. But…if the malignants scale the wall, run to the gate. We won't have time to wait if opportunity comes."

Chapter Thirteen

I slid out of bed three days later and listened to Kira complain the entire time I fought to dress myself. "I need to see the others. To make sure they're all right."

"If the governor sees you up and about, he'll proceed with the wedding." She planted her fists on her hips.

"There are far worse things than marrying Fawke." We'd discussed marriage before, but delayed planning it until after the war with Soriah. So, the wedding got moved up a bit. There were far worse things to worry about. Like escaping this place.

Dressed in the hated gray dress and coverings, I asked Kira to accompany me. "It'll be less conspicuous with two of us. If we walk slowly, maybe no none will spare us a glance."

"There are guards outside, Crynn." She shook her head. "They won't allow you to go anywhere without the governor's say-so."

"Fine." I stepped outside. "Fetch the governor."

The two guards simply stared.

"Now."

The instant they headed off, I moved toward the underground holding cells. Let the governor come to me. I probably shouldn't antagonize him, but I would face the devil himself to make sure my people were safe.

When we reached the trapdoor, Kira pulled it open and ushered me ahead of her. I glanced around, then descended the stairs.

My group was in a cell away from the others. Ezra gripped the bars. "It's good to see you, Boss."

I smiled. "Are they treating you okay?"

He nodded. "Once you and Fawke are wed, they'll let us out, or so they say. I'm not holding my breath."

"Something will come up to get us all out of here." I didn't blame him for doubting the governor. I didn't trust a word that came out of that man's mouth.

His gaze swept my face. "I'm going to kill the man who did this to you."

"Just leave the governor to me." I placed my hands over his. "Stay strong." I glanced at each of them in turn. "I will get you out of here."

Approaching footsteps had me back up the stairs to where Kira waited. As I stepped from the cellar, the governor and the two guards strode toward me.

"Satisfied your people aren't being harmed?"

He set his mouth in grim lines.

"Release them."

"As soon as I'm convinced Fawke has his team under control."

I frowned. We would all have to be very good actors. "I'd like to see him, please."

"Of course. I'll escort you, then my men will return you to your cabin when your visit is finished." His gaze flicked to Kira. "Return to the infirmary at once."

"Yes, sir." She ducked her head and rushed off, but not before I saw the flash of defiance in her eyes.

Good luck, Governor, forcing any of us to conform. Head down, I meekly followed him to Fawke's cabin. One of the guards opened the door, and I stepped inside.

"Crynn." Fawke wrapped me in his arms. "You look…very colorful." He stepped back to peer at my face. "How do you feel?"

"Like I've been kicked by a team of mules."

"Have you ever seen a mule?" He arched a brow.

"No, but I read books." I chuckled and lowered carefully into a chair. "Some of them had pictures."

He laughed and sat on the bed across from me. "It's good to see you up."

"Yeah, but I tire quickly." I removed my face covering. "I came from seeing the others. They're fine considering they're locked up." With a glance at the door, I lowered my voice. "Any idea how we're going to free them and escape?"

"Not yet. This place is a fortress from the inside." His smile faded. "Our wedding has been set for three days from today. You okay with that?"

I nodded. "Better you than him."

"Thanks." He laughed again and reached across the space between us to grip my hands. "I will find a way out, if…" He took a deep breath. "I've been hearing a lot of noise from the other side of the wall. The malignants will find a way over the wall."

"I know how to open the gate."

"Good. If they come over, you make a run for it."

"Not without the others. I'd have to free them first."

He groaned. "Okay. Find me. Whatever it takes, find me. We'll free the others together, then leave this place, taking anyone with us that wants to flee."

"Mostly women and children."

"Whoever." He tightened his grip on my hands. "You are my primary concern. Always. Without you leading the people, resolve and courage will falter."

"That's too much pressure." Tears welled in my eyes, blurring my vision. "We're a team, remember?"

"Yes, but our team still looks at you to lead them. This war can't be won without you."

I nodded and struggled to my feet. "Guess I'd better regain my strength in three days." I gave a shaky smile, knowing my ribs wouldn't be healed enough to fight if the malignants scaled the wall. I couldn't handle it if anyone died trying to protect me. "Where is our armor?"

"Guess it's with our weapons. I'm going to try and sneak out tonight and grab them. If I'm successful, I'll leave yours in back of your cabin. Wear them under that dress at all times. It might be our only defense. Getting them to our friends will be tougher."

"Try bribing a guard." At this point, anything was worth a try. "It can't cause any more trouble than you're already in. Maybe set you back in convincing Herr Governor you're on his side."

"True. The man thinks this place is invincible. If he keeps us locked up long enough, he believes we're bound to change." Fawke gave me a quick kiss at the door. "Be careful. I love you. See you in three days."

It sounded like an eternity.

On the morning of the third day, I woke to two women standing over my cot. "Time to prepare you. Bath first." One of them gripped my arm.

"I can get up myself." Pulling free, I gingerly pushed to a sitting position, hanging my legs over the side. My wedding day. I sighed and struggled to my feet.

Flanked by the two silent wraiths in gray, I made my way to the bathhouse where a tub of hot water awaited me.

No scented bubbles or skin-softening soap like the brides in Soriah indulged in on their wedding day. No, a bar of simple animal fat was my luxury. Using one of the women to stabilize me, I stepped carefully into the tub and slowly submerged myself.

The heat of the water soaked into my aching muscles, and I closed my eyes. "Let me soak as long as possible. Keep the water hot."

"Yes, ma'am."

My eyes snapped open. "Gage?"

Sparkling eyes peered down at me. "I promised to wed the Mountain Man in order to attend you today."

"You won't!"

"Of course not." She tossed me a rag. "I'm also not going to bathe you. You're quite capable of that yourself." Gage tossed the other woman a quick glance and lowered her voice. "There's no other way to walk around free. I can't wait to get out of here. This place is far worse than a pack of malignants. On a good note, our armor and weapons are lying outside our cabin. I'll fetch them tonight."

"When is your wedding?" I wet the rag and draped it over my face. The heat soothed the bruises.

"Tomorrow."

I prayed something would happen to prevent her wedding. When the opportunity for escape came, we were all getting out. No mountain man was going to keep Gage here.

"Oh, goody. You have a new gray dress to wear on your big day." Gage held a pile of folded clothes. "Even so, you'll be so beautiful."

I laughed and tossed my rag at her. "Shut up."

"At least you're marrying the man you love." Gage sobered. "I'll have to become a widow real fast if my wedding goes through." She cast another look at the other woman. "Say a word and I'll slit your throat."

The woman seemed to draw in on herself as she nodded. "Not a word if you promise to take me with you."

I stood and reached for a towel. "When the time

comes, you'll know it. Head to the gate as fast as possible, bringing anyone with you who wants to come. We can't wait for you."

"I understand."

"Until then, act normal." I wrapped the towel around me and stepped from the tub. After drying off, I donned the new gown before sitting in a chair to wait until they summoned me.

It seemed like an hour or more before a knock sounded at the door and two men entered. I stepped between them while Gage and the other woman fell in behind us. Sandwiched between my two guards, I headed for the center of the main street where the residents of Peace had already gathered.

The two men stepped back. With my heart in my throat, I moved slowly toward the front where I knew Fawke awaited me.

No music escorted me. No bridesmaids or children carrying flowers followed me. The wedding was nothing more than a farce. A grandstand for the city's residents to display my conformity, that I would no longer be a single woman. Not at all what I pictured my someday wedding to be like. All that had changed with the spin of a wheel on my eighteenth birthday.

I jerked as a malignant shrieked on the other side of the wall. It sounded like it had crossed the moat. Who would the governor sacrifice this time? Another scream joined the first. My eyes locked with Fawke's as I stepped into the open. My heart leaped into my throat, not because of the ceremony, but because the noise on the other side of the wall grew louder and louder. My hands shook as I folded them in front of me.

"Do not fear, Miss Dayholt. They cannot get in." The governor smiled at me, then at Fawke. "Today is a special day as these two not only join themselves to each other, but to the people of Peace." He reached out and took my hand, then Fawke's. Before he could announce us husband and wife, a woman screamed.

I glanced over the governor's shoulder as a malignant's head appeared. It opened its mouth and shrieked, the sound chilling my blood. Then another and another joined the first.

Fawke shoved the governor to the side and grabbed my hand. "Run!"

Chapter Fourteen

Fawke dragged me to where he'd stashed the weapons. I quickly ripped off the dress and donned my fighting clothes and armor. "We have to reach the others."

"Does Kira and Gage know where to meet us?" He tossed me my sword, then loaded himself with the weapons for the rest of our group.

"By the front gate." I took off at a sprint toward the underground jail cells. Before we reached them, two malignants blocked our path.

With a warrior's cry, I swung my sword, decapitating the one closest to me while Fawke disposed of the other one. More monsters raced toward us. Loaded down as Fawke was, most of the fighting would fall to me.

"We're here!" Gage and Kira sprinted our way.

"You were supposed to wait for us."

"Hush and give us our weapons." Gage held out her hands. "You need us."

We did. Fawke handed over their weapons. "We're going to be cornered underground." He whipped around to fight. "It'll take all of us to win our freedom."

The air filled with screams as the residents of Peace fell under the gnashing teeth and slashing claws of the malignants. My throat clogged. We wouldn't be able to free nearly as many as I'd like. I sent a quick prayer heavenward for the safety of the helpless.

"Kira, you and Gage find the children, please." I faced her, tears in my eyes. "We can't leave them to the fate of those monsters."

"Are you sure? You need us." Gage shook her head.

"We'll be fine once we round up the others, right, Fawke?"

"Sure." He didn't sound convinced as he grabbed my arm to turn me back toward the trapdoor. "We'll see the two of you soon."

I could feel his eyes on my back as I yanked the trapdoor upward. "We forgot to grab the key!"

"I've got one." A man dashed toward us, two malignants right behind him. He tossed us the key as he fell.

"Take the kids out." Fawke raised his sword above his head and went to the fallen man's rescue.

With no time to think of Fawke fighting alone, I plucked the key from the dirt and thundered down the stairs.

"What's happening?" Ezra gripped the bars.

"Malignants scaled the wall." I unlocked the cell. "Your weapons are up top. Go up there and help

Fawke."

Without a backward glance, my group rushed to his aid while I freed the rest of the prisoners. The ill man on the cot waved a weak hand. "Leave me be. There's no way I can walk out of here."

"I'll carry you," another man said.

"No. I won't let you risk your life for a dying man. Just close the cell and let me die in peace."

I spared a moment to grasp his hand. "I promised to rescue your daughter. Rest assured that I keep my promises." *Please, lady, be at the gate.*

"Then I can die knowing she's free from this place." He closed his eyes and turned to face the wall. "Thank you."

"You're welcome." I patted his shoulder, then hurried to help my friends who'd been surrounded, as they huddled at the top of the stairs. I ordered the civilians to stay in the cellar until we cleared the way, then make a beeline for the gate only stopping to bring along their families. There was no time to bring anything else.

A malignant leaped, sinking its teeth into the shoulder of my armor. I screamed and shoved it away, plunging my sword into its gut. Black, rancid blood spilled and soaked into the dirt. Another strike removed the creature's head.

We fought and killed and still more came, swarming like an army of ants. How long had they been working on finding a way in? The smell of human flesh had to have been the driving force. Where was the army? Was the governor dead, or had he found a place to save his own hide?

My mind whirled as I fought to clear a path to

the gate. One of the soldiers who had joined us fell, quickly overrun by the malignants. A few of the city's residents sped toward us armed with sticks and farming tools that were no match for sharp teeth and claws. They'd be slaughtered.

"Fawke!"

He spun around, eyes wide. "No! Goto the gate." He waved his arm at them.

A few heard and darted back the way they'd come, the others stampeded.

Yard by yard, we fought our way closer and closer to freedom.

My arms ached from swinging the sword. Sweat poured down my back. My breath came in gasps.

I slammed my riot shield into one of the creatures, shoving it back. Dante speared it through the heart. The air filled with the grunts and shrieks of battle. If we didn't get out soon, we'd fail. Exhaustion weighed heavy on my limbs and etched on the faces of my friends.

"We have to leave."

Fawke nodded. "We run."

As one, the group stepped out of our back-to-back fighting format and headed for the gate as fast as our tired legs would carry us. Occasionally, we'd have to stop and fight, then resume our mad dash once again.

Gage and Kira fought valiantly at the gate, keeping the malignants back as women, children, and a few men staggered through the gate.

I glanced around the crowd. No sign of the governor or Mountain Man. No matter. I'd return at a later date and dispose of them. We joined Gage and Kira forming a half-moon circle around the gate and continued fighting until all who wanted to leave had passed through.

"I'll close the gate and duck through. Go." Dante reached for the lever.

"No. Come with us." I reached for him.

"I'm the fastest." He gave me a shove, knocking me into Fawke, who pulled me along after him.

The gate started to close behind us. We stood our ground, killing and knocking the malignants who squeezed through into the moat.

Dante's riot shield protecting his head and neck, he sprinted down the rising gate, diving over the moat before the gate closed with a thud. He grinned, shooting to his feet, and kicked one of the monsters, sending it over the edge.

"We did it!" Gage fist pumped the sky.

"Don't let your guard down. We aren't out of this yet." Fawke blew out a breath. "We need to transport these people safely to the compound. That field of tall grass is still in front of us."

"Rest first." I leaned heavily on my sword and studied the refugees. "Who is left behind?"

A man stepped forward. "I saw some women and children fleeing to the underground cells. I tried to convince them to come, but they acted as if they couldn't hear me."

"Fawke?"

"We'll come back for them." He cupped my cheek. "I promise. Right now, these people are our main concern. We'll head to the shack we slept in the night before entering this den of hell."

I nodded. Rest came first. Food and water would have to wait until we arrived at the compound. "Fawke will lead the way. The rest of us will follow behind the refugees. Quiet is of the essence." I eyed several of the children. None of them cried, although several sported silent tears coursing down their cheeks. Had they been taught to be stoic at such a young age?

My heart ached at the lives these children had lived. Hopefully, things would be better for them in our compound, although they wouldn't be as well fed. Jenkins, the man who led our people in my absence would have a fit when we showed up with thirty more mouths to feed.

We followed as Fawke skirted the field of grass and headed for the barnlike shack we'd spent a night in. As the building came into view, night descended, casting us into darkness. We had no packs of supplies or medical equipment. Nothing to ease the ache in bellies or the dryness of throats. Nothing to soften a night on hard ground.

Our only chance was for Lars to see our trackers and know we'd left the city. If he sent a drone, we could ask for supplies to be dropped off.

I slid down the wall into a heap and rested my head on bended knees. Only now could I take a few minutes to determine whether I'd been injured. Since most of the substance covering me was black, it was easy to say I was soaked in malignant blood. The smell of death filled the shack.

"Try and sleep." Fawke sat next to me. "We have a long hike ahead of us."

"Made slower by children and women who aren't fighters. Neither are the men."

"They'll learn. We saved lives today, Crynn."

"And got no closer to growing an army to bring down Soriah."

"We'll get there." He entwined his fingers with mine. "I have to admit to being disappointed that our wedding was interrupted." He bumped me with his shoulder.

I laughed. "Me, too, although it wasn't the wedding I'd imagined."

"We'll marry someday." His thumb brushed across the top of my hand. "I'd kiss your hand if it wasn't covered in black slime."

"I thought you loved me." I grinned.

"More than anything." He lowered his head and kissed me. "Thank you for not dying."

"Same to you." Without Fawke, I doubted I'd have the drive to continue the task set before us. I'd like to think I'd do it for the people, but my heart wouldn't be in the fight.

I leaned my head on his shoulder and closed my eyes, awaking to the sound of whirring propellors. Staring into the camera of our drone, I smiled. "We need food, water, and medical supplies before we start the walk back home. Can you provide these?"

The drone did a dip. Lars' way of saying yes. The drone sped away. Hopefully, we'd have what we needed by morning.

I pushed to my feet and moved to the doorway to take my turn at standing guard. Soft snores and the occasional whimper of a child followed me.

"Everything's quiet," Moses said. "Did you get

enough rest?"

"Yes. Go lie down. I've got this."

He nodded and headed for a far corner.

A faint glow lit up the distance. Not the city of Peace, but to the east of our compound. Was it fires from the army, or was something set ablaze? It wasn't close enough to warrant more than a passing thought. I'd be worried if it threatened the field of dry grass. As it was, I figured the army was burning some malignants. Good. They could stay in the east. For once, it would be nice to have something go easy.

An hour later, three drones arrived, each with a package attached. I untied the parcels and sent the drones back for more. Included in a box of medical supplies was a letter.

Really, Crynn?
We're struggling to feed the people we have.
You care too much.
Stop being soft. It'll be the death of you.
More packages coming.

Jenkins.

I chuckled at his predictability. Still, we would soon have the supplies we needed.

If any of the livestock still lived when we returned to Peace, we'd take them with us. I would never resort to eating our elderly or sick. We'd all starve first.

By morning, we had enough supplies for two days if we were careful. If we didn't run into trouble, we'd make it back in that time. Then, we'd make plans to turn right around and return to Peace and rid the city of the evil that kept the people under its thumb.

Our first strike against Soriah.

Plus, I had a score to settle. A vow to keep. Two men to kill.

Chapter Fifteen

After warning everyone to be as silent as possible, Fawke stepped out of the shack. When no shrieks came, he waved the rest of us forward.

The tall grass waved over our heads as a slight breeze blew. Angry storm clouds swirled overhead. If they dumped their poisonous burden, most of the refugees would be doomed. The rain would eat through their skin.

We might have enough protective covering for the children, but the adults would be on their own. I kept my eyes open for somewhere to take cover if it did rain. Not an easy task with the grass so high. I made my way to the front of the crowd. "Any idea what to do if it rains?"

Fawke shook his head. "Pray it doesn't. If we keep going at this pace and walk through the night, we'll make the compound by morning."

"The children won't be able to keep up. We're going to have to find a place to spend the night in the city." There would be no moat and thick wall to protect the people. "I can send Gage and Dante out to scout. Find the safest unsafe place."

"Good idea, although I don't like sending out two of our strongest fighters."

"The soldiers, then." I fell back until I stepped in-line with the two soldiers who had joined us before entering Peace, and I outlined what I needed for them to do.

"What if we run across the army?" One frowned.

"Tell them you were held behind the walls of Peace. It isn't a lie, and easily confirmed if anyone asks the governor." The name tasted bitter on my tongue. "Hurry back as soon as you find a place." I cast an upward glance. "More than hurry."

The two took off at a fast pace, veering left and disappearing in the grass. I hated letting two fighters go, but sometimes a sacrifice had to be made. Our primary concern was moving these people to safety.

We stopped at midday for a brief rest. Kira handed out strips of dried meat. Rat most likely. Much better than human flesh. I cast a glance at a woman feeding her child.

Had she known what the chicken on her plate had really been? I shuddered and stared at the jerky in my hand. I wouldn't have been able to eat had I known. Nibbling at the edge of the meat in my hand, I knew exactly what it was. A rat. A sustainable resource in our underground compound and helped stretch the chicken we did have.

"Let's go," Fawke called after fifteen minutes. "Sky's growing darker. If you've something to cover yourself with, do it now."

Women donned their scarves and head coverings, pulling their children close to their long skirts. The few men had very little with which to cover their skin. Kira handed out blankets which would help but not be enough to protect them in a downpour.

I glanced up as a drone hovered over my head, then dropped a small canvas bag into my hand. I opened the drawstring and smiled. Lars had sent antidotes in case anyone received a malignant bite.

"That man always knows what we need." Kira smiled and stared into the bag before shoving it into her pack. She frowned and pulled it back out.

"That could also mean he thinks we're going to need those injections." I swallowed against the rock growing in my throat. Seeing our surroundings through a drone gave Lars a vantage point I didn't have. Without the earpiece I'd worn before Peace took everything from me, Lars had no way of communicating with us. The injections were dropped as a message, a warning. The medication inside was precious, and Lars had sent ten.

"We must be heading into a herd." Gage fell into step beside me. "I wish there was a way for Lars to tell us where they are."

"He did." Kira handed me a note. "I found this stuffed inside the bag."

I read, *"Large herd at two o'clock and moving slowly your way. I don't think they know you're there yet, but if the wind changes—run."* No time to wait. We needed to find shelter now. I jogged to Fawke and handed him the note.

A muscle ticked in his jaw. "We'll head in the direction the soldiers went." He stuffed the note into his pocket and motioned to the others that we were turning. "Hopefully, we'll meet up with the soldiers on their return so we aren't moving blind. Waiting on word from Lars will take too much time."

With danger looming in front of us, I stayed at his side, ready to fight if need be. Other than my group, the refugees had no weapons.

A light drizzle fell from the sky, and I pulled my riot face mask over my face. I turned as women shoved children under their long skirts. The men hunched under the blankets Kira had handed them. The only good thing about the rain—it would force the malignants into hiding.

The drone arrived with another message, this one alerting us of a group of soldiers at our ten o'clock, and that Lars would let us know when it was safe to proceed. We were going to be caught in the middle. Where were the two men I'd sent out as scouts?

After an hour, Fawke halted, holding up a fist to tell us to stop. We'd come to the edge of the tall grass. A ruined city spread in front of us, the only sounds the patter of light rain and the murmuring of the children behind me.

"What about that building?" I pointed at what had once been a gas station a century ago. "The windows are broken, but it has a door."

The sudden increase of raindrops made the decision for us. Fawke led us at a fast pace into the abandoned building.

I shoved up my mask and took a deep breath.

No rancid odor of malignants. "Settle in, folks, but stay quiet. We're here until we get the all clear."

The subdued rustle of people settling on the cracked cement floor filled the air. I stood at the shattered window while Fawke closed and blocked the front door.

"I'll check the rest of the building to make sure there isn't another way in," I said.

"We might want one. If there is, find a way to temporarily block it." He leaned against the wall, his gaze locked on the street outside. "Take Ezra with you."

I nodded and waved the oldest member of our group toward me. "Let's check out this place."

Skirting a hole in the roof that allowed a waterfall of poison to flow in and form a puddle behind a sagging counter, we headed for a door hanging on one hinge. I peered inside. Not seeing or hearing anything, I shoved it open.

The door fell with a loud thud, sending dust into the air. I stifled a sneeze and froze, waiting to find out whether a malignant had been close enough to be startled by the sound.

"Good job," Ezra muttered.

I rolled my eyes and stepped into a metal room full of empty shelves. A steel door beckoned from the wall opposite us. I waved Ezra forward.

He hurried forward and turned the knob. The door swung open and revealed a dark alley. We'd found a way out if needed. He stepped back, closed the door, and engaged the lock.

I turned and led us down a short hallway. A bathroom with a shattered sink and empty toilet occupied the one to my left, a small room and an office the right. Another door led to the alley. We locked that door as well and returned to the front where the others waited for us.

I joined Fawke at the window. "Two ways out. Both locked for now."

"Good because I'm seeing shadows move across the street. Through the rain, I can't tell if they're malignant or human."

"Maybe they're our scouts."

"Maybe. My gut tells me otherwise."

His gut was rarely, if ever, wrong. I checked my sword to make sure I could easily reach it if trouble arrived, then eyed one of the guns on Fawke's hip. He hadn't been able to retrieve all the firing weapons but had managed to arm himself and Moses. Three were better than none. We'd have to steal more when we ran across a squadron from Soriah.

Two soldiers ran down the street. "Those are the scouts."

Fawke picked up a rock and tossed it, striking one on the shoulder.

They both turned. When Fawke waved out the window, they dashed in our direction.

"Good. When we couldn't find you, we thought the worst." One of them sagged against the wall, gasping. "We ran toward the city when the rain came. There is a group of soldiers hunkered down wo blocks over. One block that way—" he pointed the way he'd come, "are monsters. We barely made it here undetected."

The danger was closer than we'd thought.

"Take a rest, guys," Fawke said. "Let's hope

we can sneak out when the rain lessens enough to make it safe. The malignants won't venture out even in a drizzle."

The other soldier shook his head. "No longer the case. Their skin must be evolving because we saw several out before the rain became a downpour. They're no different than us when it comes to the rain."

I sent Fawke a shocked glance. This made things much harder. I directed Fawke's attention across the street. "They're closer than we thought."

Staring at us from the shelter of another building were the glowing eyes of at least five malignants. Once the rain slowed, they'd be on us.

"We can handle them. They can't penetrate the building except through this window."

"There's a hole in the roof big enough for one at a time."

"Then, we'll put two fighters there. We got this."

I truly hoped so. Five yes, but if more came…I grew anxious like this every time I had more than fighters in my care. That's when I started to doubt our ability. Thankfully, Fawke rarely lost confidence.

"The rain is slowing. Move those who can't fight in another room. Dante and Kira, guard the hole in the roof. The rest of you, join me by the window."

"We can fight." One of the civilian men stepped forward clutching an iron bar. "This is almost as good as a sword."

"I've got this." Another held up a piece of wood as thick as his wrist. "After the fighting lessons you guys gave us, we can do something."

Fawke nodded. "Guard the door in front of the women and children. If any malignants get past us, you'll be the last line of defense."

They turned and followed the fleeing women and children.

"We'd better not let any move past us." I pulled the gun from his belt. Shooting would alert any soldiers of our location, but it was also the easiest way to dispose of monsters.

Moses handed one to Dante. "I want that back when this is over."

Dante grinned. "Find another one. This is mine now."

Chuckling, Moses came back to the window.

We formed a line—Fawke, me, Moses, Ezra, and Kira. Weapons in hand, we waited. We didn't have to wait long. The rain slowed to a mist. Five malignants stepped from the building. A few seconds later, another five, then another.

"They're coordinating." My breath left me in a rush as the creatures split up to surround us.

"Stand your ground." Fawke breathed heavily through his nose. "You said the back doors are locked? Other than this window and the roof, there's no other way in. Fire before they reach the halfway mark. Focus on those who are closest, then try and pick off those on the outskirts."

I nodded and took aim. What we didn't shoot would be upon us seconds after their comrades fell.

"Ready…fire." Fawke fired, my shot following a breath later.

Two malignants fell. I aimed for another and

missed as it went down on all four. Shrieking, they galloped toward us.

Fawke and I fired again and again, finally drawing our sword. A gun blasted behind us as a malignant tried getting through the hole in the roof. A child screamed from the back room. The sound spurred the monsters to move faster.

The first one lunged through the window. I lifted my sword and impaled it through the chest, taking us both to the floor. We rolled until I could get my legs under me and thrust it off my weapon. It hunkered, then leaped again, its teeth coming inches from my neck.

I'd been bitten before, but a bite to the neck would rip out my jugular. There was no injection to fix that type of wound. I screamed and shoved again, then stabbed my sword into its heart.

As the creature hung over me, the light left its eyes.

Foul blood covered me.

Other monsters moved past outnumbering my friends. Fawke and the others formed a fighting circle, forgetting the window and the roof. We were in complete survival mode now.

I struggled to my feet and joined them.

Chapter Sixteen

Outside the building, gunshots rang out. The enemy soldiers had joined the fight. Instead of running the malignants off, they swarmed into the building.

"Looks like Soriah hopes these things will finish us off…with the soldiers' help." Ezra grunted and swung his sword.

"Don't…stop," the words tore from my tortured lungs. Every swing of my sword was a monumental task. "We…will win."

Keeping the optimism was our only chance. Once we disposed of these creatures, we'd have to fight the soldiers. A new burst of adrenaline kicked in. I gave a primal yell and fought harder, jabbing and swinging, disposing of monster after monster until I leaned, heavy against Ezra.

"No time." Fawke raced past me. "We must get the people out the back before the soldiers come in."

We all turned in unison and charged after

Fawke into the room where the refugees huddled. Fawke locked the door behind us, then made a beeline for the door that led into the alley. He turned and faced the crowd. "We have to run. Carry the children if you have to. Everyone stay quiet. We will run until we find a safer place for you, then we'll leave you there so we can't fight the soldiers."

Exhaustion lined his face, but I knew Fawke would not quit, would never quit, as long as he drew breath. He stepped into the alley and waved the people forward.

How long until the soldiers entered to see whether any of us still lived? Kira wove in and out of the fighters to assess any wounds, then joined Fawke and me at the front.

"Dante is bitten. We have to find a place for me to tend him."

"There is no place." Fawke blew out a breath. "If he can walk, give him the injection. We rest when we're home."

I didn't like the decision, but I understood. One man—even one we cared about—wasn't as important as the group as a whole.

I tapped Fawke's shoulder and pointed to a building looming above the others. "What about there? We can head upward, disposing of any threats as they climb up behind us. It's worked before."

His gaze followed mine. "Take Ezra with you and check the place out. We'll be following. Come back if it isn't suitable." He grabbed my hand as I turned to go and pulled me close, planting a kiss that felt desperate on my lips. "Be careful. I can't lose you."

"You won't." I caressed his cheek, then went to grab Ezra.

"You and me again, uh, kid?" He checked his weapons. "No one I'd rather head out with."

"We share that sentiment." I grinned and jogged toward the tall building a couple of blocks over. With malignant blood coating both of us, we wouldn't be easily detected by the creatures. Staying undetected by the army was our main concern at that point.

A shriek sounded from inside a building we passed. I froze, my hand reaching for my sword. When nothing attacked, I continued. Ezra stayed at my side.

"We should probably nab a couple of soldiers if we can and take their guns."

I shot him a quick glance. "That's a big risk."

"Not if they're scouts. They'll be away from the main group and easy pickings." His teeth flashed through the grime on his face. "We haven't raided in a long time. They'll have supplies."

"The group is waiting for us to return."

"We check out the building, leave a sign, then find a couple of soldiers on their own." He wouldn't be deterred, and the idea did hold merit.

If we determined the building safe, what would a slight detour matter? Ezra was right about us needing supplies such as weapons and medicine. I nodded. "Okay, but only a short raid. I don't want to leave the group without our protection for long." We needed a much larger raid. Something similar to when we'd infiltrated the army camp. We couldn't win against Soriah without guns.

The day fell quiet, the only sound the occasional scuff of our boots. Birds flew overhead, promising someday life would return to a new normal. The first time we'd seen birds in the mountains at Jenkins' camp, I'd thought I hallucinated. Now, the crows provided some variety in our diet, laying eggs in their cages deep underground in the compound.

Ezra pulled my attention away from the sky. He pointed two fingers at his eyes, then across the street where shadows moved behind the broken windows.

We weren't alone.

Increasing our pace to a run, we ducked around a corner, plastering our backs to the rough concrete wall. "Malignants or human?"

Ezra shrugged. "No idea, but since we haven't checked out the building Fawke is leading the others to, we can't find out. Come on." He pushed away and darted toward our goal.

We slowed as we approached the towering building. I peered inside, then stepped into the dimness.

Concrete steps led upward from a cavernous room empty of everything but fallen ceiling tiles. Not smelling anything but dust or hearing anything but my own breathing, I headed for the stairs, leaving Ezra to watch my back.

All four of the following floors were the same. Fallen ceiling tiles, chipped columns, a shattered window…and only one way up. The stairs. Perfect to pick off attackers. I peered over a railing that let me see all the way to the bottom floor. We'd taken refuge in such a place before and lived to see another day.

I bent and wrote a message in the thick dust that we'd gone on a raid, repeating the same message on the first floor before heading back to the street. Time to investigate what we'd seen one block over. Besides us, there could only be two living species out there. Malignants and soldiers. We hadn't seen another human outside our group in a very long time until coming upon Peace.

After a short search, we found a back way into the building in which we'd seen movement. Inside, I paused long enough for my vision to adjust and listened for sounds of life.

Hushed whispers reached my ears. Human. Good. Ezra might get his wish of procuring supplies.

Watching where I placed my feet, I moved forward. The soft glow of a fire emanated from around the corner. As we moved closer, I detected five different voices, then a woman begging to be let go.

I shared a serious look with Ezra. Our raid had turned into a rescue mission. Slowly I removed my sword from its sheath with my right hand and the gun with my left and tossed it to Ezra. "Move slow," I mouthed.

Ezra nodded.

I squared my shoulders and stepped around the corner. Five men huddled around a fire. A woman dressed in the gray of Peace and teenage boy, hands bound in front of them, sat a few feet away.

It took a few seconds for the men to notice us. When they did, they bolted to their feet and reached for their guns.

"I wouldn't." Ezra aimed at the closest soldier. "I've got a twitchy finger. Wouldn't want to accidentally shoot one of you. Hands up and backs against that far wall."

The woman and boy scrambled to their feet and came to stand behind us. I quickly cut through their bindings. "Gather those packs and their guns. Bring them to me."

The two nodded and rushed to do my bidding. When they had completed the task, Ezra nodded at the soldiers. "Now, we usually ask those we come across to join our cause, but men who take a woman and kid against their will are not the caliber of people we want with us. So, my partner here is going to take this woman and kid away from here while I dispose of you."

So, he chose to kill them. I could stop him, being his leader, but I agreed. These were not the type of people we wanted with us. Nor could we let them return to the army. "Make it quick and quiet," I said, loud enough for them to hear.

He nodded.

I ushered the woman and boy to the front room, doing my best to ignore the pleas of the five men. Soon, no sound came other than that of Ezra extinguishing the fire.

"We'll go through the packs back at the other building," he said after joining us, his arms loaded with knives and swords. "These two look like they'll fall down if they don't get some rest." He stuffed the weapons into a tattered backpack.

"We're fine," the woman said.

"You don't look fine." I jerked my head toward

the door. "You can tell us how you came to be in their clutches when we're safe. We move fast and quiet." I recognized the boy as one we'd trained. "Ezra, hand him a sword."

"You sure, boss?" He narrowed his eyes.

"We might need him." I met the boy's startled gaze. "You remember what I taught you?"

He nodded and accepted a sword from Ezra. "I remember."

"Good." I studied the area outside, then led them back the way we'd come.

Fawke met us at the entrance, his gaze falling on the woman and boy. He pressed his lips together and blew sharply through his nose. "A successful raid, I see."

"We haven't gone through the packs yet, but I'd say we were successful. The others?"

"Upstairs."

"Any trouble?"

He shook his head. "We managed to skirt around the army. I can't promise they won't find us, but for now we're safe."

Upstairs, I sent our newcomers to Kira to check them over, then I sat next to Dante. "How are you feeling?"

"Like I've been bit." Sweat glistened on his brow. "It's my left hand, so we're good. Kira said all I need is a good night's rest."

"Thank goodness for the antidote." I clapped him gently on the shoulder, then went to question the woman and boy.

"I tried to get out the same time you took the others out, but I couldn't find Ryan here. By the time we forced the gate open again, you were gone. We tried to find you, but the soldiers found us first." She pulled her son close.

"You left the gate open?" I frowned.

"We had to. There was no one around to close it." She paled. "Those things are still inside."

"Did you see any of your people?"

"I saw several of them heading for the underground cells."

Just as we'd suspected. They wouldn't last long down there without food or water. "You're safe now. We'll take you to our compound. Your son will be trained as a fighter."

"Against Soriah?" A look of eagerness shone on the boy's face.

"Yes." I waited for his reaction.

"Good. I hate them." He lifted his chin and glanced at his mother. "I won't take it back."

"I'm not asking you to." She smoothed his hair away from his face. "I'm not exactly a fan either."

"Can you tell us why Soriah has chosen this path?" I motioned for Kira to bring them food and water.

"The president has a new group of advisors. Men who told him of a better way to increase the human population." She exhaled heavily. "Peace was the experiment."

"Soriah has followed that same path. What happened to Sharon, the president's right hand?"

"She's been imprisoned for refusing to conform when they took away her role."

I peered closer at the woman, recognizing one of the governor's wives who had opened the door when I'd banged on it.

I smiled, sensing a possible ally in Sharon, a woman who had once been my enemy. Nothing opened a person's eyes like losing everything.

Chapter Seventeen

Seven soldiers approached the building at night, doing their best to stick to the shadows. Since I'd been on watch for an hour, my eyes had adjusted. Shadows didn't move.

I nudged Fawke awake. "We have company."

He woke in an instant and reached for his weapon. "I'll wake up the others."

Nodding, I returned to the window in time to see the soldiers slip into the building downstairs and out of sight. No problem. They'd have to come up the one set of stairs to reach us—easy pickings.

I slowly pulled my sword from its sheath and waited. Silent as wraiths, the rest of my group gathered around, all clutching their weapons. The boy—Dirk, I think his mother called him—stepped up beside me with a sword in his hand.

"Not this time, buddy." I jerked my head toward his mother. "You stay back there and help guard the women and children."

"I want to fight."

"Protecting them is every bit as important." I put a hand on his shoulder. "I'm trusting you to do that. Can you?"

He nodded and backed up.

Fawke's warm gaze landed on mine, and he smiled. "You're good with kids."

Maybe, someday, I could be good with kids of my own. I returned his smile and peered over the stair railing.

The men below climbed two-by-two. One hissed as another scuffed his boot against the stair.

The other man shrugged. "They know we're here. I guarantee it."

I glanced at Fawke, then moved to the top step.

"You're right. We know you're here. Stop where you are and drop your weapons."

The clatter of guns filled the air.

"Don't shoot." The one in front raised his hands. "We aren't here to fight. If you're the rebel group, we want to join you."

"How do you know who we are?"

"We branched off from the group headed to Peace to kill off those…things. We don't want to fight for Soriah."

"Why not?" I moved next to Fawke.

The man's eyes widened. "Because of you."

I raised my brows. "That requires an explanation."

He turned and waved someone forward. "This is my wife. Because of Soriah's new laws, she can't be a soldier anymore. She'll be sent to Peace or Soriah and forced to live as a slave. None of us think women should be treated that way."

I caught the arrogant look of another man who smirked my way. That one would be trouble.

"Come on up, one at a time." Fawke stepped back.

As they came, our group separated them and kept guard over them. Except for the man and his wife. Fawke and I led them away from the others where Fawke ordered them to sit against the wall.

"Won't the rest of your squad know you're missing?" I kept my sword ready. One wrong answer, and this man wouldn't live to see tomorrow.

"Yes, but we slipped out while fighting malignants." His face fell. "I hated leaving them like that, but I can't let Lynn have to live under the new rules."

Tears filled his wife's eyes. "We thought we were fighting for a better world. Not what this one has become."

I could understand. "Any of your group you don't trust?"

Lynn glanced at her husband, who nodded. "Tad. The man sitting behind you to the left."

I glanced back. The arrogant one. So, my gut instinct had been right. "Why did he come with you?"

"So he wouldn't have to die under the claws of those things. Tad doesn't see anything wrong with the new rules. Says he plans on taking at least five wives. He was looking forward to reaching Peace."

"He'll be disappointed. There isn't much left. Malignants scaled the walls."

Lynn gasped. "Are they all dead?"

"We don't know for sure. Once we're able to formulate a plan, we'll head back and rescue whoever is left. My apologies, but we'll have to tie your hands for now." I motioned Dirk over and asked him to fetch bindings and hand them to each of our group.

"We understand. I'm Olson," the man in front of us said. "You'll find supplies in our packs. Help yourself."

"Thanks." I jerked my head for Fawke to join me once the husband and wife were tied up. "Do we take them with us?"

"Yes, but we blindfold them when we're close. Until we know we can trust them, I don't want them wandering around our compound." He glanced at Tad. "Especially that one. I don't like the look of him. When we leave here, we don't stop again until we're home."

We headed out at first light. Lars sent a drone that flashed a rudimentary map on its screen to show us the safest route before it flew away.

"Impressive," Olson said. "No wonder you've managed to evade capture."

Not really. We'd been prisoners of Peace just because we needed to recruit fighters for the upcoming war. Lars hadn't been able to warn us about that.

We'd stop for a few minutes here and there to let the women and children rest, drink some water, and nibble dry meat. Sometimes, we'd stop because of nearby malignants, but most of the time we pressed onward. A few blocks from home, we blindfolded the soldiers.

When the fallen Ferris wheel came into sight, the tension fell from my shoulders like a gentle breeze. Underground, we were safe. Not even Soriah's bombs could hurt us there. Whoever had built the amusement park and its many tunnels had been a genius—a lifesaver they hadn't even known they were.

Jenkins had opened the heavy steel door before we arrived. "About time you travelers made it home." He grinned.

"Any trouble?" I brushed past him.

"Not a one." He glanced past me. "Looks like there's more than I thought."

"Picked up a few strays along the way. Those with their hands tied need to be contained for a bit. The others need rooms." I descended the stairs and into my mother's arms.

After a hug, she set me at arm's length. "You had me worried."

"It'll take more than a crazy man to stop me." I gave her another quick hug. "I could eat an elephant."

She laughed. "I'll make sure you're all fed. Go get cleaned up. You don't smell so good."

I told Fawke I'd meet him in the dining room, then headed for the showers. I set my dirty clothes near the door. The cleaning women would know they were mine. I stepped under the welcome hot spray of water.

Leaning one hand against the wall, I closed my eyes. Only now did I let the fear and worry from the last few weeks overcome me. In all honesty, I hadn't expected to make it back home. Not in one piece anyway. Especially after realizing the malignants were trying to find their way into Peace—a city with only one way in and out.

Not wanting to waste a precious resource, I cut off the water and dried off with a towel hanging on a nearby hook. With the towel wrapped around me, I went to my room where I donned the simple cotton top and pants I wore in the compound, the same "uniform" most of the others wore. But, that too was starting to be in short supply with every new person we brought in.

The dining room was empty when I entered, but a large round table had been set up in the center of the room. A large platter of eggs, mystery meat, and vegetables occupied one end. A map filled the center.

I peered at the faded blueprint preserved by Eb who had died a few months back. He'd lived in the compound for decades, taking care of everything his grandfather had built.The map of the town told the complete story about what the city had once been . Eb had marked the location of the compound and other important landmarks. I traced a road to where Peace was located. It had once been a small man-made island. My finger stopped at the moat, apparently part of the city's fortress for a long time.

"Cool." Fawke kissed the back of my neck. "I wonder what other treasures Jenkins has discovered down here." He stepped to my side. "I'd like to leave in the morning, if possible. The people left behind won't survive long in those cells."

While I hated the thought of leaving so soon, I also knew we had to. We couldn't leave innocent people defenseless. By now, the rest of our group had started trickling in.

Moses sat, crossing his arms. "What's the plan?" His eyes darted from Fawke to me.

"We leave in the morning."

Everyone's shoulders slumped. "No rest, then." Ezra frowned.

"Not yet." I tapped the map. "We'll save a little time by following the straight path to Peace. Hopefully, the soldiers took care of the malignants and left."

"What if they stuck around for the residents?" Gage tilted her head.

"Then we take care of them. I also want to bring back every living animal. If the malignants didn't break into the barn and log enclosures, there would be chickens, hogs, and a couple of cows. That will make our return trip slower."

Ezra shook his head. "Foolish idea."

"We need the food with more people living here." It was a small hope that the animals had escaped the creatures, but the malignants seemed to have hatred for humans above all other things. They ate our flesh, but they often simply killed us for sport.

"I'll leave instructions to build more pens," Fawke said. "Just in case. We can hatch chickens, birth cows, raise hogs, and eat something other than rats once in a while."

"Dreamers, both of you." A smile cracked Ezra's face. "But I'll play along. Let's get those critters. How many people we taking?"

"Us." I nibbled the inside of my cheek. "And volunteers. The more we have, the better the chance of success. I might be optimistic about livestock, but not about the soldiers or malignants. One of them would've remained behind."

"You aren't leaving me this time." Jerome marched toward us, his dark face set in determination.

"Be glad we did. You'd have been locked in a schoolroom where we are. But, you can come this time." Any of the younger ones could help with the livestock.

"I'll have Lars make an announcement for any volunteers to meet us here at breakfast." Kira headed for the door, glancing back before she left. "You are going to let us eat again, right?"

I laughed. "Absolutely."

"I'll have the kitchen prepare supplies." Gage headed away from the table.

"That leaves us men to take care of weapons and chicken cages." Ezra pushed to his feet. "There's a lot to do before bedtime."

"Don't leave until you've eaten." Gage and Kira would return with us. "We need all the strength we can get." I filled my plate and sat, moving the map out of the way. I shared the same sentiment as the others. I would've liked to have stayed a few days, but there were innocent people to save.

Chapter Eighteen

Two days later, we stood once again at the edge of the tall grass. The change this time was the lowered gate, too burned to be raised. I doubted we'd find anyone alive inside.

"I'll go first." Fawke stepped forward. "Once I'm across, follow single file, leaving a few feet between each person." He cast a warm glance my way and set foot on the bridge. He marched across with confidence, then waved the rest of us forward.

I joined him in case we were attacked from the city and waited for the others to join us. As one, we entered Peace. It had become a ghost town.

Not a single person walked the street. Doors hung off the hinges of houses. Smoke rose from ashes of buildings burned to the ground.

"Let's head for the cells. Stay alert. Put the cages down. We may not need them." Fawke kept the lead.

Jerome and Dirk, the only teens in our group,

dropped the chicken cages and replaced them with swords. Jerome could face any danger, but I wasn't sure about the other boy. Hopefully, I wouldn't have to take his body home to his mother. I moved closer to the boy.

The barn still stood with all windows and doors closed. I smiled as a flicker of hope that the livestock had survived grew within me.

We made as little sound as possible as we headed for the underground cells. Fawke sent me below, staying up top with the others. It only took one to unlock the cells, and I had held onto the key given me the last time I'd been down there.

The murmuring of multiple voices reached me. My boot scraped against the stair. The murmurs hushed. A breath later Mountain Man stood at the bottom and glared up at me.

My fingers curled around my sword. I wasn't defenseless this time.

"Step back, William." The governor took his place and grinned up at me. "I wondered how long it would take for you to come rescue us."

"I'm not here to save you. Only your people." I stared around him at the eager faces of men, women, and children. Maybe twenty in total. So few? "Is this all of you?"

"Alas, it is. Those monsters disposed of the others. We tossed their bodies in the moat, after a prayer for their souls, of course."

"Of course." How was I going to rescue the people without the governor and his henchman? There was no way I would take those two to our hidden compound. I'd figure it out later. There'd be a whole day of traveling to devise a plan. "Let's go. Take only what you can carry."

"Can we grab things from our homes?" A woman asked.

"You have ten minutes. We cannot tarry." I marched back up the stairs and let the others know the governor was still breathing.

Fawke made a noise in his throat. "We'll figure something out. If we take him, he'll let Soriah know where our compound is."

"We can't let him live." I watched as the people filed up the stairs and scattered to gather whatever they could find. "Let's gather the livestock and meet at the gate." I put two men to stand as lookout and headed for the barn.

Moses and Ezra pulled the heavy doors open. The putrid smell of death greeted us along with the snorts of hogs, the cackle of chickens, and a moo of a cow.

I moved further inside to find a bull dead in a stall. The apparent sign of death was the gash across its throat. The poor beast had managed to make his way into the barn after his attack. Someone had then closed the doors.

"Jerome and Dirk, catch the chickens, then herd the cow and hogs to the gate." It would be a big job, but I had faith in the boys. "I'll send you help in a minute." The refugees could make themselves useful by helping with the livestock.

I stood at the gate and waited as refugees joined me with what few belongings they could carry, mostly clothes and dishes. "We don't need the dishes. What we do need are medical supplies, food, and fabric. Bring all you can. Make it quick. The longer we remain, the bigger our chance of discovery."

Shoulders slumped, but they dropped their things. Several of the women turned and headed for either the infirmary or the kitchen.

"Those creatures left the day after you did." The governor rubbed at a spot on his shirt. "As far as they know, there is no one left here."

"You were wrong about them once before, remember?" I narrowed my eyes. "Because of you, people died."

"Mistakes happen, Miss Dayholt." His eyes flashed. "Live and learn, isn't that what they say?"

I rolled my eyes and stepped away from him. The man soured the very air around him. I ordered three of his men to help with the livestock.

"Incoming!" Gage pulled her gun and fired into the herd of malignants galloping our way.

Women and children shrieked, dropping the supplies they'd gathered, and made a dash for the underground cells. When the governor and Mountain Man started to follow, I shook my head. "You stand and fight. Every man and woman without a child fights. Grab anything you can."

The governor paled. "I have no fighting skills."

"That's bad news for you." I unsheathed my gun and joined in the firing. We wouldn't be able to drop all the malignants, but we should be able to make their numbers more manageable. I'd never seen such a large herd before.

"These things were lying in wait." Dante shook his head. "Waiting for signs of life. They *are* evolving."

Which chilled my blood. Thinking, planning, malignants were far worse than mindless killing machines.

"Stand your ground," Fawke ordered. "We can pick them off as they cross the bridge. Do not pull back except on my command."

"What do we do?" Jerome called out.

"Guard those animals." They were every bit as important as the people. Both human and livestock were essential to build a new world.

Any talking ceased as fighting and staying alive took all precedence. From the corner of my eye, I spotted the governor picking up a pitchfork. I whipped around as the man came toward me rather than the creatures swarming through the gate.

An evil gleam shone in his eyes as he faced me. "No offense, but I have my orders."

I spared a glance to locate his massive sidekick. The giant had become overrun by malignants and was slowly forced to his knees. I felt no remorse over his end. I wouldn't feel any over the governor's death either.

"Sorry, but I do take offense." I jumped back as he jammed the pitchfork toward me. "You had opportunity before. Why didn't you take it?"

"I foolishly thought you and Fawke would see our ways were the right ones. Since you haven't, I've been ordered to kill you. With their leader gone, the others will come around to Soriah's way of thinking."

"Is the president really that stupid?" I arched a brow, slowly circling him while I waited for an opening. "Someone will simply take my place."

"There is no more spinning of the wheel."

I frowned. "Do you actually think that without a wheel to appoint a new leader, one won't step forward? That is no longer how it's done. No longer the way my people think." Or anyone given the chance to think for themselves.

"Without you and your foolish rebellious ideas, they will." He lunged forward. "Soldiers are coming. I notified Soriah this morning when one of my men spotted you coming through the grass."

Plunging my sword into his gut, I yanked the pitchfork from his hands. I leaned forward as he fell, and I pulled my sword. "These people are now free." I planted my boot on his chest and pushed him over. With one last contemptuous look at him as the light faded from his eyes, I went to help the others dispose of the malignants.

When no more came through the gate, we'd lost two men and a woman. Her child, a small girl around the age of three, peered up at me from the bottom cellar step.

I held out my hand. "Come on, sweetie. Let's get you out of here." When she came up, I put her in the care of another woman and led the group back to the gate. Without speaking, they gathered up the supplies they'd dropped, barely sparing the governor's body a glance. I guessed he hadn't been as loved as he'd thought.

Kira treated the bitten and scratched. We didn't have the luxury of giving them time to rest. Not with the governor's warning. If the army caught us, me and my group would be executed or imprisoned. I couldn't let either one of those happen.

I told Fawke what the governor had said.

He nodded. "We'll have to go quick. These people either keep up or get left behind." He shouted orders over the group, then led us from the now fallen city of Peace—a place inhabited by nothing more than ghosts.

The only sound as we moved through the tall grass were the sounds of the livestock. I tensed at every moo from the cow who badly needing milking. None of us had the energy for another battle.

After a few hours, Fawke called a short break. The refugees huddled in the middle while my group formed a circle around them. My sword felt like it weighed fifty pounds in my hands, but I could still swing it if I had to. I'd fight until my last breath for my people.

I'd been truthful when I'd told the governor someone would step forward as leader if I fell. Most likely Fawke or Jenkins. Jenkins had already successfully led a village until choosing to follow us underground and join the rebellion.

After a few bites of dried food and a few sips of water, Fawke ordered everyone to their feet. "Until we reach our destination, we don't stop. We can rest there."

Without complaint, the people pushed to their feet, hoisted their supplies onto their shoulders, gathered their children close, and followed. When we cleared the tall grass, Fawke paused.

I scanned the buildings for signs of life. No shrieks, foul smells, or shouts of alarm.

Fawke waved us forward.

"Doesn't this feel too easy?" I asked him. "If the soldiers were coming, wouldn't we have noticed them by now?"

"Yes. I'm fearing an ambush. Keep everyone close."

"Should we turn back? Go somewhere other than the compound?"

"And what? Slowly starve to death? Our supplies won't last until morning, much less days or weeks."

My skin prickled as I fell back, spreading the word among the fighters. An ambush would finish us off. I refused to let Soriah win. My heart fluttered as the Ferris wheel came into view, and my steps quickened. We'd arrived at our destination without being attacked.

Again, Jenkins held the door open, his eyes widening at the sight of the animals. "Can't say as a cow will do much good underground, but I reckon she'll make good fertilizer for the vegetables."

I laughed and clapped him on the shoulder. "We're building a new world, my friend. She'll adjust to life underground the same as we did." I descended the steps into safety.

We'd wait to see what tomorrow would bring. For now, rest waited for us all.

Chapter Nineteen

Everyone in the dining room grew silent and stared as I entered three days later. I searched the room until I met Fawke's gaze. Something had happened.

"What?" I glanced from face to face.

"Grab your oatmeal and come with me."

My mother rushed forward and thrust a bowl into my hands. "It'll be fine."

I frowned. What in the world was going on? What had I missed by staying in my room recuperating from the last few weeks? "Thanks." I followed Fawke's broad back.

He led me to the control room where Lars spun around the second we entered. "This isn't good, boss."

"Can someone please tell me what is going on?" I stared at the bowl in my hand, appetite gone.

"Eat. You're going to need your strength." Fawke gently moved me in front of the bank of monitors. "We were followed."

I jerked my gaze from him and focused on the screen in front of me. Three soldiers hunkered behind a pile of debris. "How do you know they followed us?"

"I heard them talking." Lars exhaled heavily. "Once they noticed the drone, they shot it down. They know we're underground; they just aren't sure where our entrance is."

"Let's take them out before they alert the rest of their army."

"There were five of them an hour ago." Lars shook his head. "We're about to be in a battle."

Knowing Fawke was right about needing my strength, I downed a spoonful of oatmeal. "There's time to prepare. We move the women and children deep into the tunnels. Those who can fight congregate in front of each entrance."

"What if they use bombs?" Lars tilted his head.

"This place can handle them. Don't forget that Eb's father and his group lived down here when the bombs went off that destroyed the city above us."

"Poison?"

I shook my head. "Their goal is to expand Soriah. They won't pollute the place again."

The whole purpose of the Stalkers, of which I'd been appointed leader, was to rid the city of the monsters so Soriah could rebuild. Unfortunately, no one expected the creatures to breed like rabbits or evolve into reasoning beings.

"They do want my head on a stake." Something I did not intend to give them. "We don't know how long we have before they attack, so training resumes in earnest. Do we have any more drones? I'd like you to sweep the city."

"Only one with the capability of going far enough. I'll have it ready in an hour." Lars opened a cupboard on the opposite wall.

"I can't believe we were foolish enough to be followed." Inhaling through my nose, I released a breath slowly out my mouth.

"It couldn't be helped traveling with women, children, and animals." Fawke motioned his head toward the door. "Time to fill in the others."

"From the way everyone looked at me when I entered the dining room, I assumed they knew."

"Only that something was up." He placed his hand on the small of my back and guided me back to the dining room where most of the compound's population waited for us.

I set my empty bowl on a table and took a deep breath before facing my people. "Our home has been discovered." I held up a hand to still the gasps and cries. "We'll be okay. This place is impenetrable."

"We thought Peace was too," a man shouted. "Look what happened there."

"This isn't Peace. We have fighters and steel doors. Those who can fight will meet in one hour in the main hall. Women, you will prepare the rooms in the tunnels for habitation for a few days to a week's time." I didn't see a fight lasting longer. Once the clamor of battle ensued, the malignants would come out of the woodwork. The soldiers would be sitting ducks.

"We are sending out a drone to estimate how much time we have, which won't be a lot. A day or two at the most. Quick preparations will be key. Do not fear. The army will have to go through steel doors, then our fighters before reaching you." I would not let that happen while I still drew a breath.

Soriah would not dispose of the civilians, necessary for its survival. My group was not and would be executed. I dismissed them all and headed for the armory to prepare for the fighting lessons until Lars let me know the drone was ready.

Staying busy would keep me sane as the responsibility for these people weighed on me. I'd left Soriah at the age of eighteen to lead a group of seven. At the age of nineteen, I led a group approaching a hundred. I'd never felt more inadequate in my life.

"I see the doubt on your face." Fawke stopped me in the hall and turned me to face him. "You become like this every time the people are in danger, yet you'd face danger alone without a second thought."

"Being responsible for others is big." Maybe too big for me.

He pulled me close and nestled my head on his chest. "I'll tell you the same thing I've told you a hundred times. You're a natural leader. These people love you. You've done a good job, Crynn."

"Blah, blah, blah." My words were muffled against his chest which shook with silent laughter.

"Come on. Let's do something you know you're good at. Teach others to fight."

"Crynn to the control room, please." Lars's voice rang over the intercom.

I sighed and stepped back from Fawke's

comforting embrace. "Let's see what we're up against."

Lars turned to face us when we entered the control room. "I've let the drone loose through the back door. Let's fire it up." Lars sat in front of the monitors, Fawke and I taking our places on each side of him.

I watched as a drone lifted into the air, flying high over the three soldiers just outside the boundary of the amusement park. Malignants glanced up as the drone flew over their heads. Lars sent it up one street and down another. All was clear for at least a mile.

"Maybe those three soldiers are deserters."

"No, Boss. They wouldn't have shot the other drone down if they didn't have evil intent."

True. Fine. I'd stop grasping at straws. The danger to the compound was grave despite my display of bravado in the dining room.

"Here we go." Fawke leaned closer to the monitor. Two tanks, followed by a crowd of soldiers, rolled down a street a few blocks further on.

"How long until they reach us?" I straightened. We had a tank we'd stolen, but one was no match for two. If we could steal those two, we'd have a greater chance of success when we attacked Soriah.

"Two days, maybe three, depending on how packed with debris the roads are, and whether the soldiers combine forces with malignants." He exhaled slowly. "That's enough time for us to be ready for them."

"I still say we need to dispose of the three out there. The less information they can relay back to the army, the better."

"Okay. We'll head out at dark." Fawke turned to leave, then glanced over his shoulder. "Find some people to keep working on clearing the additional exits. We might need an escape route."

The tunnels we'd discovered a few months prior snaked in all directions under the former amusement park. Heavy debris blocked several exits. Whoever ventured out to clear it would be in danger.

"Post guards. If those scouts move closer, bring our people in." I glanced at Fawke to see whether he'd argue. When he didn't, I stepped into the hall.

While the days weren't much lighter due to our polluted atmosphere, the world was now noticeably darker when the sun set. The world was beginning to heal after Soriah's desperate attempt to gain control by eliminating all outside its walls.

Together we headed for the armory to gather our weapons before joining the fighters in the great hall. Men, some women, and teenage boys awaited our arrival, all armed with wooden swords. I glanced from face to face, knowing that all of them might not survive this fight if we had to take it outside. All I could do now was prepare them the best I could.

The rest of my group each took a few of the volunteers in the room, and soon the air echoed with grunts and the thuds of wood against wood. We stopped for the noon meal, then resumed until dinner. In the morning we'd gather again.

"I know you have a plan," Ezra said the moment I sat down with my meal.

I chuckled. "We're going out at nightfall to dispose of the three scouts. We still need whatever weapons we can grab. But—" I waved my fork. "My larger plan is to steal those tanks once we defeat this army."

"That's a big plan." He crossed his arms and grinned. "I like it."

"You're that sure we'll win?" Gage frowned and shook her head. "How big is the army?"

"Maybe fifty." I filled my fork with mashed potatoes.

"How many tanks?"

"Two."

She blinked a few times, then nodded. "Doable."

My group's optimism filled me with hope. I definitely couldn't do what I did without them. I trusted every one of them with my life.

"You're both crazy." Dante dug into his meal as if it was the last one. The scar from where a malignant had bit him on the shoulder appeared raw above his collar. "I say we wait and let the malignants take out as much of the army as possible, then we swoop in."

"I didn't say we were attacking the army tonight." I arched a brow. "Just the three scouts."

"What do you think, Fawke?" Moses pushed his plate away. "You've been quiet on the subject."

"I agree with Crynn. The three scouts have to be taken out. Then, we wait for the army and prepare while we wait." He finished off his meal. "We train, we eat, and we rest as much as possible. We've all been through a lot lately, and I don't want anyone falling behind because they're tired."

Heads nodded.

I smiled, shoving aside my apprehension.

"We've been in tougher situations than this and come out the victor. Don't forget Peace."

Gage scoffed. "How could we ever forget about that place? I almost had to get married! Not to mention malignants saved you and Fawke from saying 'I do.'"

I smiled over at him. "We wouldn't have minded too much if the wedding had gone through."

Fawke returned my smile and placed his hand over mine. "Someday."

"Someday." At a time and place we chose. The mountain where we'd met Jenkins and his people would be perfect.

I pushed my empty plate aside. "We've a couple of hours before dark. I don't anticipate spending the night out there, so bring water and wear your riot gear. Don't forget night-vision goggles. We want the element of surprise."

Chapter Twenty

I pulled my googles into place and shoved open the exit door. The world outside lit up with an eerie green light. I waited to hear any shouts. When all remained quiet, I stepped out and waved the others forward.

Fawke grumbled about me going first as he joined me. I grinned and motioned for us to circle around in order to approach where we'd seen the three scouts.

"Lars?" I pressed my earpiece.

"All clear so far. The main army has stopped to pitch camp. I guess they aren't expecting anything from us."

"Thanks." The army's first mistake. We hadn't survived this long by not acting when the moment struck. "Stay with us."

"Will do, Boss."

Fawke moved ahead to lead the way despite my telling him not ten minutes ago that I would go ahead of the group. Shaking my head, I followed. The man was impossible.

Staying below the line of debris, we moved at a quick pace until we reached the edge of the former amusement park. Hopefully, when the army arrived, the outer exits of the compound would be accessible. We could then make an attack from several directions.

Right now our mission was simple—to dispose of the three scouts and grab their weapons and any other supplies they might carry. We were little more than scavengers at this point. Fighting would come later.

Fawke held up a fist to stop, then pointed two fingers to our right. I listened, catching a hoarse whisper. With a nod, I veered in that direction. If the army had sent out multiple scout groups, our job would be a lot harder.

A small fire flickered ahead. Idiots. I raised my goggles, pulled my sword, and stepped into a clearing in the middle of piled cement blocks and concrete.

"Hello, boys. You asking for company? Because that fire guarantees you'll get some." I glanced at the small gas flame.

Two men bolted to their feet, hands raised. "We were hoping you would find us." Their eyes widened as the rest of my group moved into sight.

"Oh? Why?" I held the tip of my sword under the chin of the nearest man.

His Adam apple bobbed. "We're deserters."

"Unhappy with the new Soriah rules?"

He started to nod and thought better of it. "Yes.

My wife and daughter are back there. I don't like the way they're being forced to live."

"What do you think I can do about it?"

"Word is that you're staging a rebellion."

I lowered my sword. "Sit and tell me what you've heard." I motioned for Dante and Moses to keep their weapons trained on the men. "Start with your names."

"I'm Don and this is Lee. He's a widower with two small daughters."

Okay, so far I could see why they might want to leave the army. "Go on."

Don frowned as Fawke covered the fire with a slab of concrete. "I overheard our captain talking to Mal about—"

"Who is Mal?"

"The man who took Sharon's place once the new rules took effect."

I nodded for him to continue.

"Mal told the captain that his primary goal was to take out the rebels. So, the captain sent out some scouts who followed the group." He shrugged. "Then, the group disappeared."

I glanced at Fawke. The army knew the general proximity of our compound but not the actual location. Good. "What else?"

"That's it. When the army made camp, Lee and I took a 'bathroom' break." He made finger quotes. "We brought some things to help you decide whether you want us or not." He jerked his head toward a crate.

"Ezra?"

"On it." He pried the lid open and stepped back

with a whistle. "Guns, ammo, grenades, smoke bombs…you name it, Boss, we got it." He dug in the crate. "And a few medical supplies."

"We would've brought more," Lee said, "but that's all I could grab. I used to be a nurse before the army took me."

"Can the two of you fight?" I returned my attention to them.

"Yes." Don squared his shoulders.

I hunkered down in front of him, locking my gaze with his. "We're going to take out three scouts. Are you going to have a problem with that?"

"Only if they don't surrender peacefully. There are more of us wanting to defect than you know."

"Can you send a message to them?" If they'd defect now, before the upcoming battle, we'd gain a foot forward. "You could both return and invite those wanting to join us to meet here in this spot—same time tomorrow night."

He glanced at Lee. "It'll be dangerous for us, but yes, we can do that."

I thrust out my hand. "Welcome to the rebels." We'd find out for sure whether he told the truth. If those waiting for us tomorrow night attacked, we'd fight. Otherwise, our army would grow. "We'll take the supplies. Thank you." I pushed to my feet.

He stared at my hand for a moment before returning the shake. "We'll be here. If we aren't, it's because we're dead." They snatched their guns and took off in the direction of the army.

"Can we trust them?" Gage narrowed her eyes.

"They gave us supplies. Even if they plan on an ambush, we still have these. We'll pick them up on the way back. I doubt this next three will be as friendly when we arrive." I pulled my goggles back into place.

"You sure about this?" Fawke asked.

"We have to grow our army any way we can. Recruiting soldiers is the best way and faster than training novices." Time was running out.

Dante moved the crate behind a pile of cement, then we headed in the direction of the army scouts. I hoped we wouldn't have to kill them, but the chance of them also wanting to join us was slim. We couldn't be that lucky.

No fire burned with these scouts. Instead, they huddled against a chipped brick wall, arms tight around their waists. Their guns lay beside them. No whispers passed their lips. These three did not want to be found. Not by us anyway.

This time I didn't step into view alone. All of us stood this time without a word.

The men leaped up. Cries of alarm escaped their lips as they reached for their guns.

"I wouldn't if I were you." Fawke aimed his weapon. "Kick the guns closer to me, then kneel with your hands over your heads."

The three soldiers glared, the complete opposites of the two we'd just met. They kicked the guns over and did as they were told.

"You going to shoot us right here?" One of them spat.

"That's up to you guys." Fawke slid the guns to Moses. "Grab their packs, too."

"As in what?" The man asked.

"Whether you're going to come with us

peacefully or not."

"You gonna eat us like those people over in Peace did?"

Heaven forbid. "No. If we kill you, we'll use you for fertilizer in our garden. Make your decision now. Peacefully or fodder?"

"Peacefully," he growled.

"Ezra, bind their hands, please."

The soldiers grumbled as their hands were tied, but they came along, albeit grudgingly, as we left their hiding spot. Once we were away from the threat of malignants, we'd have to blindfold them in case one of them escaped.

Despite the familiarity of this scene, the hair on my arms stood at attention. The night's quest had been too easy. Something wasn't right.

"Do you feel it, Fawke? The uneasiness in the air?" I stopped.

"Yes." He studied the area around us. "I can't hear the tanks. There aren't any malignants screaming."

A thrumping sound came from the sky. I widened my eyes as a flying machine flew closer. What was that?

"Hide!" Fawke shoved me.

We sprinted for the nearest building.

"What is that?" I leaned against the wall of a small brick building.

"Helicopter." One of the soldiers grinned. "We can track you from the sky now."

"A plane." Ezra slammed the butt of his gun into the soldier's stomach. "How many do they have?"

"One right now, but they've found someone who knows how to repair the old machines." He grinned. "Soriah will be ready for you."

Ezra turned. "Can I shoot him, please?"

"Not yet." I paced the small space. What could we do against…helicopters? I shook my head. I'd been an avid reader before leaving Soriah, and I'd never even seen a photo of any machine that could fly.

I wasn't worried about the machines discovering the compound. Nothing above ground hinted at what lay beneath. What worried me was our ability to leave the compound. I'd rather confront the army away from the women and children.

Fawke exhaled heavily. "Let's make it back quick. We'll hide whenever that machine gets close. When we're safely underground, we'll decide how to handle it."

"Okay." With a wary glance at the sky, I stepped from the building and pressed my earpiece. "Lars, we need you to alert to things like flying machines."

"It came on me too fast. I wasn't expecting anything in the air other than my drone."

"Can you see it now?"

"No. I'll do a quick search."

I hung up as Ezra plunged his sword into one of the soldiers. I pulled mine from its sheath. "What happened?"

"The dude went for my gun. He's untied." Ezra shook his head. "A shard of glass from the window."

"Either of you want the same treatment?" I stood in front of the other prisoners.

They shrank back, shaking their heads.

"Great. Being good boys will keep you alive." Keeping my sword in my hand, I led the group from the building, keeping a vigilant eye on the sky.

A block from the amusement park and out of sight of the Ferris wheel, Gage blindfolded the soldiers. "I'll try not to trip you, but no guarantees." The man yelped as she tightened the strip of fabric over his eyes.

"Women fighters are cruel."

"Boo-hoo." She gave him a shove. "Start walking. You're tethered to your buddy."

Fawke waved us forward. Twice we stopped and hid when the helicopter flew overhead.

When the Ferris wheel came into view, some of the tension left my shoulders. Only a little farther and we'd be safe.

I spoke into the earpiece for Lars to have someone ready to open the door. "We're coming in hot." I could already hear the whirring blades approaching. The empty amusement park lot didn't leave anywhere to hide. "Run!"

We sprinted for the hidden door. Jenkins had it open before we reached it and took possession of the two soldiers.

At the bottom of the steps, I faced Fawke. "It's only us two who will greet the defecting soldiers tomorrow night. If it's a trap, we'll return back here immediately."

Chapter Twenty-One

The rest of the group argued until I gave in. They were waiting at the exit at the appointed time.

"The compound needs you guys here." I shook my head.

"The compound is safer than we will be." Ezra glared. "You need us in case things go sideways."

I did, but I still wanted them to protect the people. "Fine. Let's make sure we're back before the army launches its attack."

"It's not exactly as if it'll be hand-to-hand combat," Gage pointed out, hooking a gun holster to her belt. "It's all going to be done by rockets and bombs. We're of better use out there."

I knew that, but I still felt as if we needed to be here in the compound with the people in case the worst happened. "We'll be back when it all starts." I wouldn't leave the people alone.

"We'll be back." Fawkes clapped me on the shoulder, then opened the exit door. "Lars said the army is close, so it's silence from here on out."

A cold wind blew, a frosty reminder that winter was on its way. The only thing good about the bitter cold coming was that it helped mask the foul odors of the city. I shivered and followed Fawke away from the compound.

The door closed behind us with a heavy thud. I prayed we'd all make it home. Without me and Fawke, I feared the residents of our compound would simply surrender. Soriah would win.

We trudged along in silence, moving carefully across debris. Occasionally, Fawke would pause to assess our surroundings. Sometimes, we'd hear from Lars. Other than that, nothing but the wind sounded through the darkness, lit only by gas fires in the distance.

Someone behind me tripped and sent a rock clattering into a brick wall. We froze, moving on when no shouts of alarm came.

Where were the malignants? Hiding because of the strength of the approaching army? It made sense to me. I'd do the same if I was only responsible for myself. Why would I even enter a battle where the odds were stacked against me?

The location of our rendezvous with the defecting soldiers was now only half a block away. The sounds of the army—the crunching of tank tires, the clattering of weapons—filled the air. They were too close for comfort.

Every nerve in my body twanged. My palms sweated. If the defectors did join us, our group would double in size, making it harder to escape undetected. I checked to make sure my gun was within easy reach. Swords would not be our first choice.

Fawke motioned for us to halt, then waved only me forward. "We move ahead alone," he whispered. "We'll send out whatever defectors wait for us one by one. The rest of you head back in small groups once they reach you. A large group will alert the army to our presence. We'll meet back up half a block from our back entrance."

"Got it," Moses said.

They melted into the shadows.

The back entrance would add almost an hour to our return trip. I slowly pulled my gun and stepped around the fallen concrete wall where we were to meet up with anyone wanting to join us. That's when my mouth fell open.

At least twenty soldiers awaited us. All wore heavy backpacks and carried multiple weapons. The one we'd spoken to earlier stepped forward.

"We're here. There might be others, but they're late."

"We can't wait," Fawke spoke barely above a whisper. "In groups of three, you'll join one of our groups on the other side of this wall and head for the compound. When you get close, you'll be blindfolded and held in a cell until we know we can trust you. Anyone want out?"

No one said they did, so Fawke sent the first three on their way.

My heart lodged in my throat as the artillery sounds grew louder. "This is taking too long," I said. "We need to leave." The only good thing about the noise was it masked our own.

Fawke nodded. "Move faster, folks. You know

the consequences for deserting if you get caught."

Finally, the last few soldiers headed off with us. Half an hour later, we met up with the others who had congregated in an alley.

"Large herd of malignants ahead," Ezra said. "We thought it best to move as a group rather than a few at a time. Hopefully, our size will scare 'em off. If not, we'll fight them."

And possibly give ourselves away to the approaching army. I nodded and moved to the front of the group. "Maintain silence from here on out."

The cadence of over twenty footsteps echoed. It would be a miracle if we arrived at the compound undetected by human or monster. I peered around the corner at the end of the alley.

A cracked asphalt street stretched in both directions. Gas fires broke up the darkness. The rumble of the tanks grew in the distance. Clouds played peekaboo with the moon. Time was running out.

I pressed my earpiece. "We need eyes, Lars."

"Okay, but it's risky. If they see the drone, they'll know we're close."

"We're blind." I motioned for the others to stay in the safety of the alley.

Only eyes could detect us there. No tank would be able to get through. If we stayed in the dark and remained silent, the foot soldiers might pass on by.

Fifteen minutes later, Lars spoke again. "Army two blocks to your right. Large herd of malignants between you and them. That's good news for you. The army will have to head in another direction or take care of the monsters first. In the meantime, you should get a move on. The army won't hear you."

"Thanks." I waved the others forward then sprinted across the street. We would keep to the alleys before having to move out into a less covered area.

It didn't take long for gunshots to pierce the night. The ground shook with an explosion. It wouldn't take the army long to clear the way. I increased my speed, the others thundering after me.

The sound of gunfire hid our movement. When the shots slowed, so did we. I didn't want to take any chances of others hearing us over the noise of the tanks' tires. Right now, according to Lars, the army didn't have a firm grasp on our location. I wanted to keep it that way.

Someone cried out behind me. I turned to see a soldier help his comrade to his feet. The man who had fallen couldn't put pressure on his left ankle. I stifled a groan and signaled to Kira to check him out. An injured person would slow us down.

Time ticked away, and the enemy grew closer before Kira filled me in. "It's a sprain. He'll do further damage if he walks on it."

"He has to walk on it. Get two of his buddies to help him. Tell them we can't wait for them. They'll have to keep up."

She nodded and rushed to let them know.

I stepped from the alley and came face-to-face with two startled malignants. They bared their teeth, then sniffed the air, before galloping away. Whether frightened by our number or the army's, they didn't seem to want any part of us.

My heart rate slowly returned to normal, and I

dashed to yet another alley. This would be our last cover before ducking behind piles of debris on our way to the amusement park.

Once at the edge, I clung to the shadows the best I could. Those behind me formed a long line. I hoped they could be trusted. There was no way we could blindfold them and reach safety quick enough.

Fawke jogged to my side. "Tank lights at ten o'clock. We need to step up our pace quick. There's no way to do this without them seeing us. Our best bet is to get as close to the exit as possible and make a run for it."

"I'll alert Lars to have someone open the door for us." Just then the artificial gleam of headlights broke through the shattered walls of a nearby building. We weren't going to make it. "Run!" I waved for the others to go ahead.

No longer worried about silence, they darted across the amusement-park lot to where Jenkins waved from the back exit. The door was big enough for the entire group to enter at once.

The two soldiers with their injured friend took longer.

The tank's lights were growing brighter. "They're going to see us." We needed to divert their attention.

"Crynn!" Fawke's shout followed me as I raced toward the tank.

I couldn't let them locate the compound. Right now, they only had an idea. It would be disastrous for them to know for sure.

Without turning around, I knew Fawke followed me. No way would he let me go alone. I pulled my gun, knelt behind a pile of asphalt and concrete bricks, and fired.

The first soldier to top the next pile dropped. Then another, until too many of them swarmed for me to pick off. Not even Fawke's shooting could make a dent.

"Come on." He grabbed my hand and sprinted for the nearest building. "We'll lead them away."

Bullets kicked up the dirt at our feet.

Lars's drone sped past our heads.

I grinned at the two small bombs strapped to its undercarriage. We might succeed at this after all.

The next shot sent the drone spiraling, flying erratically toward the army. The two bombs released before the drone fell. An explosion sent several soldiers flying.

Good job, Lars. Too bad we didn't have a whole lot more of the drones. We might be able to win this war without leaving the compound if we did.

"We're almost there." Fawke kept his pace to mine. I wasn't a slow runner, but his longer legs still ate up the distance much faster.

A shot rang out behind us.

Fire burned across my ribcage. The next bullet buckled my leg. I slipped from Fawke's grip and fell.

"Go on without me." Nausea rose in my throat, so intense I wretched.

"Not a chance." He put my arm around his shoulders and hefted me to my feet. "I'll never leave you behind."

With a lurching gait, we continued toward the safety of the buildings. My breath came in painful gasps.

"They'll still find us, Fawke. They've seen us. There is nowhere for us to hide."

"I have a surprise for you." He continued to drag me along until he came to what had been a gas station a long time ago. "In here."

We squeezed through the opening of a garage.

"Here." Fawke pulled up a metal door and revealed a shallow concrete pit. "It isn't much, but it's all we have. Get in. Hurry."

Outside came the pounding of running feet.

I slid into the pit.

Fawke climbed in next to me and pulled the metal door over us.

Chapter Twenty-Two

I bit down on my fist as Fawke pressed his hand hard against the wound in my side. Tears poured down my cheeks.

He put a finger over my mouth.

"I know they came this way," someone said.

"They must've gone out the back." Footsteps passed us.

After a few minutes of silence, Fawke slid the door over us to the side and climbed out. "I need to assess your injuries."

"I'm fine." I gritted my teeth as he pulled me from the pit.

"No, you're not." He peeled off my armor and lifted my shirt. "The bullet's still in here." He moved his hands slowly down my body, pausing at my left thigh. "Just a graze. We really need to get that bullet out."

"This isn't exactly the place." My eyes took in our location.

"You need medical attention." He peered out the door. "We need to get to the compound." He pulled a rag from his pack and tore it into strips, then bound my wounds.

I hissed as it pulled the fabric tight. "That would take a miracle." I leaned against a dust-covered counter and concentrated on my breathing. No amount of counting would take the pain in my side away. If we didn't extract the bullet, I'd have infection to add to my list of woes.

"Well, I happen to believe in miracles." He returned to my side and again put my arm around his shoulder. "We'll go nice and slow. The army has moved on a bit. We can make some progress."

"Leave me, Fawke." I gripped his arm. "It's suicide to take me back to the compound. Don't risk you or our people."

His eyes flashed. "I'd risk the world to take you back, Crynn. I'd rather die out here with you than live there without you. Don't you get that by now?"

Neither one of us wanted to live without the other. "One of us has to survive to lead our people against Soriah."

"Both of us will lead them." He moved me to the door, then outside. After a few tense minutes, we turned in the direction of the compound.

I didn't see any way for us to make it across the massive lot without them spotting us. The army would follow us and know exactly where to drop their bombs. I thought briefly of sending Fawke to fetch Kira to tend to me, but others needed her medical expertise. We had no other choice but to try and make it back if he wouldn't go by himself. More than likely, we'd both die on that amusement-park lot.

I gasped as we stumbled over a deep hole in the asphalt.

"Sorry." Fawke tightened his grip on me.

The pain must have addled my brain because it took that long for me to realize that the hand around his shoulder was slick with blood that wasn't mine. "You're hit."

"It's just a scratch."

"Your shoulder, Fawke!"

"I said it's fine. It's no worse than the graze on your leg." He helped me up and over a pile of fallen timber and shattered concrete. "The doctors can care for both of us once we make it back."

If we didn't bleed to death first. "Let's at least bind it. I have a rag in my pack."

"You're the most stubborn person I've ever met."

"Ditto." I shrugged off my pack and let him dig out the rag. It wasn't easy with my one hand and the darkness masking his injury, but I finally tied it enough to stop the bleeding.

"Look at that." Fawke stopped at the edge of the lot.

My brows must have disappeared into my hairline. The soldiers, fighters, and civilians marched across the lot toward the army.

Fawke put two fingers to his lips and let out a shrill whistle.

Ezra came sprinting toward us, Lars' drone right behind him. "We were sure worried about the two of you. Looks like you got into some trouble."

"We did." Fawke jerked his head toward our people. "Jenkins leading them?"

"Yep. We thought we'd cut them off before they reached us. Pick off as many as we can and take the tanks." He whirled and cursed as the top of a tank appeared over the rise. "Too late."

"Move the people back inside." Fawke led me as quickly as my stumbling gait would allow toward the back door of the compound. "We'll find another way."

"They know without a doubt where we are now." I swallowed against the boulder in my throat and prayed the compound was as strong as Old Man Eb said it was. It would have to withstand a barrage of bombs.

"No, they don't. We exited out one of the tunnel doors. If we head back in that way, they won't know for sure."

Ezra dashed back to the others. As one, the group turned and raced back the way they'd come.

"I'll have medical ready," Lars said through my earpiece. "Just get inside." The drone buzzed away.

The nausea increased as we moved faster. Adrenaline fueled my legs. I'd collapse once we were inside. *If* we got inside. I kept my eyes locked on the entrance. No way we'd make it to the tunnel door. We had to go in now.

Slowly the back door lowered. Fawke's mother and mine waved for us to hurry.

From the back of the compound, the door was hard to see. That would all change once the army made it over the rise. With what strength I had left, I pulled free from Fawke's hold and forced myself into a run.

"We thought we'd lost you." Mom dragged me into the cavernous room where we kept our one and only tank along with a few jeeps. "It's straight to the infirmary for both of you." She pressed the button to raise the wall.

I'd never watched something move so slowly before. The noise of the approaching army grew louder as the door inched upward. When it returned to its place with a muffled thud, my strength reserve failed me.

My legs gave way, and I crumbled to the floor.

The war had come to us instead of us taking it to Soriah.

Dust fell from above us as the first bomb fell.

The End

Stay tuned for The Fight, the conclusion of the Nightfall series.

www.cynthiahickey.com

Multi-published and best-selling author, Cynthia Hickey, writing as Cynthia Melton, has taught writing at many conferences and small writing retreats. She and her husband run the publishing press, Winged Publications, which includes some of the CBA's best well-known authors. They live in Arizona and Arkansas, becoming snowbirds with two dogs and one cat. They have ten grandchildren who keep them busy and tell everyone they know that "Nana is a writer."

Follow me on:
Amazon
Bookbub
Facebook

Fantasy
Fate of the Faes
Shayna
Deema
Kasdeya
Fate of the Faes boxed set

Dystopian

<u>The Wheel</u>
<u>The Hunt</u>
<u>The Others</u>

Post Apocalyptic

<u>The Darkening</u>